BLACK DOVE

A NOVEL

ROBIN WYATT DUNN
SCARLET LEAF
2017

ISBN: 978-1-988397-44-3

PUBLISHED BY SCARLET LEAF
PUBLISHING HOUSE

Toronto, Canada

By the same author

Books

Forthcoming, *Wine Country*, poetry
Forthcoming, *Sunsborne*, poetry
Forthcoming, *Black Dove*, a novel
City, Psychonaut
Colonel Stierlitz, a novella
White Man Book
Conquistador of the Night Lands
Poems from the War, narrative poetry
Julia, Skydaughter, a novella
Last Freedom, a collection of short plays
A Map of Kex's Face
Fighting Down into the Kingdom of Dreams
Line to Night Island, a novella
My Name is Dee
Los Angeles, or American Pharaohs

Chapbooks

Koreatown
Mary
Hanblečeya
Be Closer for my Burn
Telegrams from X County
A Picnic in England
Drive Thru Poems

Feature Films

A Wilderness in Your Heart

Party Games

American Messenger

Part 1
Rachel

1.

This story is not one that I thought I should tell. So much got in the way of it—but that doesn't matter. No story is easy; I know that much.

It started at a party. I was acting fifteen again, because I had gotten drunk the night before for the first time in five years. The woman who stopped me from being a complete jerk was standing in the doorway between the kitchen and the long, extended living room, and she said,

"What are you doing?"

Her tone was friendly; I wasn't used to that. Living in Los Angeles for a number of years gets you used to people being mean. I don't mind.

She didn't either; her name was Rachel. Rachel from Mossad.

It sounds funny when you say it. And maybe, in some parallel universe, it even is funny. Though this love story, like probably all love stories, is not ultimately a comedy.

\- - -

Los Angeles is an angry city. I've only been here for five years, so I don't know what it was like before that. Probably it's been angry for a while.

My friend Jake is forty years old. He looks pretty good for forty, not too fat, not too skinny, not too mean. Already that's pretty good for forty. He's not as rich as he should be at forty, though that doesn't mean much anymore since no one has any money. He's not as smart as me, but no one holds that against him. And he's funny.

"Hey, asshole, why are you holding my whiskey," he says to me when I find it in the kitchen, and takes my drink out of my hand.

In Israel they're killing a lot of Palestinians. I mean, a whole lot of them. It makes you nervous, I guess. When you kill a whole lot of people. One of those habits it's tough to break, like alcohol.

I had one drink and then a second and started in on my third when I decided it would be a good idea to start shouting about some of my opinions:

"Israel is all Nazis!"

I sat in the corner and nursed my hangover when I saw her again, reaching over the sink, in her short skirt. She had on a thong and it covered her sex in a very inviting way. As she stood back up, she turned and saw me looking. In her look is everything I love about Israeli women, which can ultimately be summed up this way: they look at you like they want to kill you, and would enjoy doing it.

She was talking to a skinny idiot in a narrow tie and then I realized it was Jake.

I stood up and leaned over to them, my head a delicately balanced bowling ball.

"Robert, this is Rachel. A neurosurgeon at Cedars Sinai."

"Wow, what a job," I said.

She smiled and went back to talking to Jake. I wanted a cigarette so I went outside.

A minute later, Rachel walked outside and stood next to me, and held out her hand for a cigarette. I didn't have one so I gave her mine.

"I work for Mossad," she said.

She took a deep drag on her cigarette and then handed it back to me.

"Thanks for that," she said, and then went back inside. There was lipstick on the filter. I took the last drag and tasted her lips.

2.

In my dream, she was crawling through the bushes, and I felt I sensed her, hovering near my body in my sleep.

She was enormous—and seemed part cat—leaping through space over me, turning to look at me in midair, with wide eyes.

I awoke and dragged myself to the shower to rinse off the sweat. I had a meeting with new clients this morning and didn't want to go. All the glad-handing, smiling and ass-kissing to pay my exorbitant rent.

I didn't see her again for two months, by which time she and Jake were dating.

\- - -

The lawn was the brightest I'd ever seen—like someone had exposed it to intense nuclear radiation. Chernobyl grass.

"You wouldn't believe what I paid for this," Jake said, coming out to meet me, here in this terrifying new subdivision.

"I found her the other day clipping roses. I couldn't believe it. A neurosurgeon, and also a gardener!"

"I think I'm going to quit," I said.

"Quit? What do you mean? You're self-employed!"

"Yeah, sort of."

"What are you going to do?"

"I'm gonna go to Russia—see the old country. Maybe bring back a new girlfriend, huh?"

"Right."

"I want to turn Russian. Become Commie."

"Sounds like a good idea."

3.

And then she asked me to go to Mexico. And I did.

It's not fair that some people should have such power over us—that they've accumulated more gravity than the rest of us. Or maybe what I mean is that I don't know why I followed her—it wasn't the sex appeal of her voice or even her promises. Fate, if you like. Fate, and gravity.

I awoke at midnight to the squeals of the wheels on the Inter-Californias train. We were stopped in the middle of the Mexican desert. She was gone. I stood up and stared out the window into the night. The stars were beautiful. Anything can happen in the night.

I stood up and walked towards the back of the train, to the dining car.

She'd shown up at my flat and told me to come with her. How often that must have happened in human history. A woman decides to leave, and companions materialize from thin air.

4.

I can recover nothing but fragments of the crash.

Light and noise—I was thrown through the air.

I heard her voice, and the clatter of plates.

I was gone, somewhere in my head. No one could take me back. And, more deeply, I was, after the crash, in those moments after, more profoundly alive than I had ever been. And, I came to understand, I was now in a different kind of world. One with different kinds of consequences.

"Are you all right?" she said, in her beautiful Israeli accent. Without a scratch.

My head was bleeding.

She tore her shirt before I could say anything, poured her canteen over me, and wrapped her rag around my head.

"Is everyone dead?" I asked.

"Come."

- - -

We walked through the desert. She walked like a survivor—now we both were. But she had already been. Each step barely there at all, ready for infinity.

"What happened?" I asked.

"There was a crash."

"Where are we going?"

"There's a town up ahead."

The light was a dull purple—perhaps an hour from dawn.

We walked and the sun rose and we kept walking. The light, and shadows, in the darkness, it felt like no one would ever come for us, deliciously. As though everything that had happened had slipped us into a dream.

- - -

She got us a room and I lay in the bed.

She was in the bathroom speaking on the phone.

I stood up and went to the window—a red car was parked outside—a new SUV. It had surprised me about Mexico—how many new cars they had. My image of the country had been stuck in the past.

I knocked on the bathroom door. She was speaking Hebrew.

5.

I returned to work. I explained I had been ill, though that did not explain my desert tan.

I stared at the computer monitor, a headache resting inside my neck and under my forehead. The world went away. The screen floated in front of my vision. The numbers on it. 34, her age. I turned it off.

Outside, the wet hot night. A woman all her own. Curved and solemn and bright. In bed I couldn't sleep.

6.

Israel. Improbably, snowing. Some Orthodox Jews moved over the yellow stone in the twilight, the snowflakes falling around them.

I bent into an alcove and put a cigarette in my mouth. It was cold. My breath came out of my mouth in plumes.

I'd caught the first flight out.

The weight of history does not rest on the shoulders, but in the eyes—every surface accounts for it. It is in the feet too. We feel it in the Earth.

In the square, an old woman moved slowly south with her bags, head covered. The scarf over her head, her jacket, the stone, and the darkening city sky of Jerusalem all the same shade of grainy yellow and black.

I lit the cigarette and thought about Rachel. Ridiculous to pursue such a woman. Like chasing a mother tiger in order to propose riding it. The judgment of her eyes is an indictment of the whole Earth, but part of me remains convinced—the male part—that it is judgment of me alone and I must change her mind. However I can.

I see her then, walking with a man. Both of them in black. I put out the cigarette and go out to meet them.

- - -

I shook their hands and smiled. Rachel was surprised to see me.

"What are you doing here?"

They spoke Hebrew rapidly back and forth.

"A restaurant," I said. "I'm looking for a restaurant. Can you recommend one? Jerusalem seems to shut down so early."

"This way," the man said.

Underneath the moon, the stairs looked like an M.C. Escher drawing, each line of the stone stark and surreal.

The man opened a door of dark wood, and we were flooded in firelight and warm soup. Not a word of English, though I heard some French.

"I've never been to Jerusalem before," I told Rachel. She nodded, as though I had said something gauche.

"Why did you come?"

"To see you."

"How did you know where I was?"

"Your mother told me."

She smiled a bit at that.

"You own a business in America?" the man asked.

"Yes, I'm selling it. Do you want to buy?"

The man laughed. "I'll buy anything." His name was David.

We ordered more soup.

- - -

I fantasized about her for hours that night. So intensely that I began to believe she was there with me, or that her mind had sent out a conscious tendril, to wrap around my own.

Jerusalem and its doors. Like most of the Middle East, the people of Israel have an intense appreciation for small spaces—the personal cave, the public cave, the private battlefield—each enclosed by a door. The first door of human history — and the first fight over it — somehow finds its echo in the city of Jerusalem. It may be that if there is a religion to unite Jerusalem, it will be a religion of doors.

She had given me her phone number after dinner (though it had been mostly me eating) and I called it now.

She had no greeting in her voicemail, only a beep. I hung up.

- - -

In some ways Israel then is a black space in my mind now — who I was, and what I did, have retreated into some fissure in my soul. Water run down into the earth. Inaccessible except by smell. I was not myself there. Or perhaps I was more fully myself.

- - -

I followed him home. I'm sure the whole neighborhood saw me following him — Jerusalem has no need of a "neighborhood watch" since that's what Jerusalem is.

The quiet street soothed me. Freshly bathed from my hotel, the night seemed beautifully alive.

"Where is she?" I asked him, outside the door.

"What?"

"Where is Rachel?"

"You don't look well. What's the matter?"

I ran my hand through my hair. "Tell me where she is."

"You should go. Or do you want a drink? I have some."

He let me inside. Through a small atrium and into a kitchen, where he poured whiskey.

"You should leave her alone. Take it easy, enjoy life. You want to meet some nice girl, I know some people. We'd like to help you."

"Where is she?"

"Drink your whiskey."

I drank it.

"I met a man when I was in America. A man like you. Someone outside the usual things. A philosopher, perhaps. Are you a philosopher, Robert?"

I smiled.

"I felt sorry for him. I think Americans are too Christian in their philosophies. Their philosophers too. Looking for the philosopher's stone. We live our philosophy here. I live it here. So does Rachel."

"No she doesn't. She hates it here."

"Maybe I hate it too. Like you can hate your mother. It doesn't matter. Why did you come? To win her? You can't win a woman like her."

"Where is your toilet?"

He pointed down the hall.

I closed the bathroom door, raised the toilet seat, and pissed carefully on the floor. When I was finished I zipped up and went back out.

"Tell me where she is."

"I'll tell her you're looking for her. You should head back to your hotel. It's dark out."

The street was silent. I walked home in the quiet, listening to my echoing steps.

Soon I would have no money. But at the moment, that didn't bother me. In the morning, I resolved, I would go to Mossad's offices, and find Rachel.

- - -

In bed, I dreamed of the ocean. I had always lived under the waves. The king was to give me his trident, but I did not want to feel it in my hands. The water in my home' country was strange and dark.

- - -

I did not make it to Mossad's offices the next morning. I was too sick to move; I called the nurse hotline and asked for some medicine. I fell asleep and when I awoke Rachel was standing over me with her dark eyes.

- - -

If I could remember why I began with her I could remember many other things I'd like: who Americans were when I was a child, and who we are now. Why we left Africa in the first place. What it cost.

We write so much about love — for so many years — and it only becomes more of a puzzle.

I watched the tiles in my room, well-crafted and worn, brown on brown. Each a small city with its routes curved round the others. I knelt down and ran my hand over the surface, along the grout and the smooth surfaces. I could hear a ghost down in there—whispering in some Canaanite tongue.

- - -

I called the boss and told him I had to postpone the article: political tensions, a lead I still needed, and money, of course. I needed money.

He sent me five grand through one of the local money changers who gave me a queer look when I asked for it in shekels.

"Not dollars?"

"No."

Outside the Wailing Wall the water sellers sang loud, and I reached for my hair, to copy the Orthodox Jews fingering their rosaries—whatever they called them.

Hair in my fingers, I called her.

"Let me buy you dinner," I said.

"Where are you?"

"By the Wailing Wall."

"I'll meet you."

The creek of life runs low at times but we are blessed by its scarce water. Her dark eyes intimate something I have never felt before—not love, but mystery.

Tell me: is this why we left Africa? For the eyes of the woman on the other side?

7.

"Mediterranean" means "Middle Earth." Israel might be Mordor. Or maybe that's Egypt?

I go to Tel Aviv for the week to stare at the sea and escape the religious energy of the capital; I turn off my phone and start drinking heavily and slow, under my canopy my eyes are half open, but my ears are wide. Listening to the waves.

We followed them all, all around the earth. Waves.

The Saxons called it the "Vandal Sea" – in part because of the tribes who settled there after Rome fell. But also because the waters are an invitation to violence.

Tel Aviv knows all about it but prefers to pretend otherwise, and that's fine with me. With enough alcohol in my system I could snooze through a small revolution.

The revolution is within me instead. I am smaller now. Newer. Somewhere inside, this child who knows me has invited me to tea:

8.

"Parasols, captain, we have them for you. Only ten American dollars."

"I only have shekels."

"Shekels? Are you a Jew?"

"No. Visiting."

"Fifty shekels!"

"Here. What's your name?"

"I'm Don Juan."

"Ha ha ha. Don, how are the ladies treating you?"

"I am conversant with them, sir, that is my business, and one day I will marry one of them, after the fall of Israel!"

"Ah, I see. When will that be?"

"Have a good day, Monsieur! This parasol, it will keep your skin healthy. Arrivederci!"

He's like a small viper, coiled and beautiful and brown. Black eyes and hair burned blonde by the light.

"Don Juan, let me walk with you. I'm a writer. Here, I'll carry your umbrellas."

"They are parasols! What do you write? Magic? I love Harry Potter!"

"No, a reporter."

"You don't look like a reporter."

"I wear a disguise."

"So do we all." He grins. He talks an aging diva out of ten dollars and hands her a pink umbrella. His brown feet are bare on the hot sun.

"Where are you from?"

"Jerusalem. And you, monsieur?"

"Los Angeles."

"Ah, Hollywood! I would like to visit!"

"Yes. How old are you?"

"Too old for you, Monsieur. But old enough for the ladies."

"Ha ha ha. Let me buy you lunch. Just to thank you for the conversation."

"I meet you later. Got to sell more umbrellas, hey?"

He tosses one of them in the air, spinning, and catches it in front of my face.

"I'll be in my office."

Soon I will melt, into the sand. The martini will aid me in this journey.

9.

I must have closed my eyes for a minute; when I opened them it was getting dark. The beach was cool and pleasant; I walked down to the water, my toes scrunching in the wet sand.

I had dreamed; there was a woman in a ticklish dress. The fabric ran over my skin. The sea is so warm. Overhead, the sky is the yellow dinge of industrial light.

No sign of my young conspirator; the beach is mostly deserted. A couple embraces in the distance. I walk back towards my hotel.

I walk up the stairs and open the door with the keycard. I step into the shower.

Is there a reason for my retreat from reality? That is, is there a chief reason?

I stay too long inside; my skin turns red.

I pick up my phone and call Rachel.

"Hello?"

"I want to see you."

"I'm busy now. Tomorrow."

"No, now."

"Tomorrow."

She hangs up. Outside, the water sellers are singing in Arabic. Such warm voices. They sound alien to my ear, but I want to sing with them.

10.

"What do you imagine you are, here?"

The cigarette looked enticing in her mouth. I wanted one.

"Me? A tourist. What do you mean?"

"No. What you represent."

"I don't know."

"You are the Etruscans, and we are the Romans. We are going to destroy you."

"Fuck me first, hey?"

"And not just you. Not just the Americans. Others."

"The Palestinians."

"No, not them. The other empires."

"Let's get out of here. Walk."

"I can't. I have a meeting. Listen: go home, Robert. What you think you are doing here, it is too innocent for me. You are too innocent. Americans too innocent. It is why you are destroyed. Go. Be happy. Go away from here."

"Maybe I don't want to be innocent anymore."

"Go."

I left her, smoking her cigarette. Looking very much the spy. I almost bought a pack, but didn't have the right change.

I watched other customers come by the stand, buy smokes, and light up. I didn't ask anyone for a cigarette, but I inhaled the second-hand smoke.

Up the street I saw the Palestinian boy, now holding a basket full of prepaid phones.

"How much for a phone?"

"My favorite customer is here!" he said. "For you, twenty dollars."

"Shekels."

"Only ninety shekels."

I purchased one and when I passed him the money I grabbed hold of his hand.

"Thank you," I said.

"Phones! Phones for everyone!" the boy shouted, moving away, up the street.

I unwrapped the device and called Rachel's number.

"Who is this?"

"I'll be at your hotel tonight."

I hung up.

Overhead, a jet was landing at Tel Aviv airport. It shook the frames of the streetside shops, an earthquake of sound. I couldn't help smiling.

11.

The night was delirious, like Vegas, only more innocent. Tel Aviv, the eternal nightclub. I rode in the back of the cab, counting my diminishing funds in my head. A few more weeks, and I would have nothing left.

The sunsets here were what I imagined 1970s Los Angeles must have looked like: deliriously beautiful. I told the cab to stop; that I would walk the rest of the way.

I watched the red sun sink behind the buildings.

I turned off my phone, both my old and new one. Outside her building, I waited.

12.

When I was a boy I always had a fascination for old things: dolls, newspapers, calligraphies of prior eras. Here in Israel, I can understand that fascination better. The root of the thing, human time, made concrete in the objects we touch. American cities are so young.

She saw me and ignored me as she pushed the buttons on the hotel door.

"Rachel."

She said nothing. She went inside, and shut the door carefully behind her. Through the window, I could see her speaking with the front desk.

These private hotels are so offensive: soon they'll go the way of Japan, and have robots for clerks.

She flipped me the bird before she went for the elevators. Such an American gesture.

I pressed the call button on the door box.

"Yes?"

"Let me in."

"Who is it please?"

"Robert Gonzales. I'm an American."

"One moment."

A guard sauntered to the front and opened the door.

He said something unfriendly sounding in Hebrew.

"Ah, yes, hello," I said. "My friend, Rachel, I'm trying to get in touch."

"Your name?" he said in English.

"Robert Gonzalez."

He spoke into the microphone on his lapel, looked back at me.

"Come in." His English had almost no accent. "You want to speak to Rachel?"

"Yes."

"You're a friend of hers?" I nodded.

"Please wait here." He retreated to the front desk and picked up the telephone.

Behind the man, art deco polyhedrons formed into a pyramid. The man gestured me to the elevator and I got in.

"Thirtieth floor."

The elevator rose quickly; I felt my ears pop.

The hallways were white, almost like a hospital. I did not know her room number; then I saw her, standing at the end of the hall. She raised her fingers to her lips. I looked at her. She gestured to the door beside her.

Then she took out her gun and fired at the lock. I thought about retreating to the elevator; she grinned at me, and made a come-hither gesture with her fingers. Like a meteor dropping into the gravity well of a swirling planet, I moved towards her. I looked into the apartment.

The boy was inside.

13.

"How did you find me?" he asked her.

He sat on the bed, legs dangling off of it.

Rachel had returned her gun to its holster under her jacket. "That's my job."

I sat down next to our Don Juan.

"He's a friend of yours?" Rachel asked.

"Yes."

"This young man makes interesting friends."

"Why not leave him alone?" I said.

"I wish I could."

"Will you let me go?" the boy said.

"This boy killed one of our men," she said.

"Did you do that?" I asked him.

"No."

"He is a spy," she said.

"So are you," said the boy.

"And why do you think I became a spy?" she asked, leaning down to the boy.

"To kill us."

"No. For the same reason you did. To protect each other."

"How many have you killed?" the boy asked.

"What do you want, Robert? You want to be friends with this boy?"

"I am his friend."

"Then you should come see what he did."

14.

I feel eternity so close to me now. But not because of Israel. Because of what's happening to me.

"My mother will be worried," Don Juan said as we rode the elevator down.

We drove to the site of the bombing.

Black blood twists over the stones; police officers interview witnesses, at the site of the blast. The boy is crying. I hold him next to me.

Overhead, a jet flies over us. A man raises his fist at the jet and a policeman shoves him back. Rachel goes to the policeman and says something to him.

I am the American witness. Behave yourself, she's telling him. Pretend.

What am I doing here?

"What are you doing here, senor?" the boy asks me.

"I don't know, kid. Let's get some ice cream."

There are one hundred flavors in the shop. Each the color of the stones of this country: yellow, red, white, black and blue. The aroma of cigarettes and coffee and sugar. I am sitting by the window, in the silence, watching the boy. Rachel comes in, and stands by our table. Her eyes are black stones.

"Sit with us."

She watches the street, and I watch her.

15.

The boy claims to follow the caliph, a word which means "successor." But I am his successor, following him, into East Jerusalem.

I am carrying Rachel's phone in my pocket.

I should go home, if only to try to forget. What I am learning.

- - -

My American passport parts the waters of checkpoints like Moses the sea. I feel the rifles watch us as we move down over the cobbled stones.

- - -

I am asleep in his home. The king of the sea holds the trident as he swims; it is turning black.

I awaken and the yellow sun has filled the room. I am in a sleeping bag on the warm red tiles.

What am I doing here?

"Breakfast, mein Herr. Here."

I sat with Don Juan's family.

The boy is like Rachel, embedded in this web I can't begin to understand. More and more I understand why people became Americans. We may be naïve, but it is a kind of genius to jettison so many centuries of accumulated pain.

"So good!" I said, putting the spicy beans in my mouth.

Outside, the sun is like Los Angeles, but harder.

"How long do you stay?" his mother asks me.

"I don't know," I said. "Let me give you some money."

"No, no," the father said. "You are our guest."

"Your boy is very strong. I want to help him. If I can. I'm in love with a woman. An Israeli woman. My life has fallen apart."

The father nods.

"You will come with me today," Don Juan says.

- - -

Jerusalem is a medieval city, but all cities are—this middle age between Africa and space. The energy of Jerusalem is like an angel fluttering in my chest, terrible and urgent.

I follow Don Juan on his rounds in this city, selling nuts and some homemade beer, which I carry in my backpack. To one market he sells the lot, and I sit on a crate in the back, light catching the dust-filled storeroom into a nest of sparkling yellow mites.

Don Juan came back into the storeroom. His eyes full of violence. I understood he was going to do something, that I should accompany him, or talk him out of it.

But I let him go and slept, like a beggar, in the storeroom, my eyes closed against all the decisions I had made for these years, bringing me here.

The Palestinians say they are defined by outsiders through violence, that their only observable actions are violent ones. All other truths, myriad and beautiful, have become invisible in the geopolitical eye.

Perhaps this is a kind of blessing, this stripping away. Deadlier than a dream is your body, made into a noose to hang the kings and the kings of kings, always more, ready for us to do the hanging.

16.

I'm coming faster now to the end. Jerusalem is also an engine, and I am being fashioned into a gear.

I am turning:

- - -

I know why the Jews came to Los Angeles. Because of the light. The light is God.

I am stumbling through the street, blinded by it. The noise of the horses and cars and the dust surrounds my head like gauze, cushioning me as I try harder to slip away . . . slip away from myself.

I spend the night in the drunk tank. When I awaken, it's Rachel. Again.

She speaks to the guard in Hebrew and he opens the gate.

We're kissing.

17.

Jerusalem and my body are in co-orbits. But Rachel is an even larger orb . . . my orbit degrades; I shall crash:

Into her sweat.

- - -

"What did the boy tell you?"

"Where to sell beer."

"Where do you sell beer?"

"In Isobel Street."

She is so heavy against me. Lead. I am light.

"I'm going," she said. "Lock the door behind you when you leave."

I wanted to sing. Or jump off a bridge. Or both. I took a shower and enjoyed the aroma of her feminine soaps. When I came out, there was a knock at the door. I opened it, towel around my waist. It was David. He looked at me, then stepped past me, into the apartment.

"Did she leave?"

"Yes."

"Do you have a drink?"

"I, um . . ."

"Never mind, I know where the liquor is. Ha ha ha."

He looked below the sink and brought out a bottle, poured it in a glass.

"It's not a problem, you and her, we don't care. Do what you like. It's just I'm concerned: what has she been telling you?"

"I should go. Excuse me, let me dress."

I ducked back into the bedroom; he followed me to the door and spoke through it while I threw on my jeans.

"I know I'm an asshole. Believe me, you're not the first person to piss on my floor! It's fine. But you know, Rachel, she doesn't usually do this. Mix work and her bed."

"I thought that's what all spies did," I called out.

"Ha ha ha. She's not that kind of spy. Nor am I. Look, I don't mean to bother. Do what you want. But call me, hmm? I leave you my card."

I heard him leave. I threw on my shirt. His card was on the table. I put it in my pocket and went outside, pulling her door shut behind me.

I could see why I wanted Rachel: she was more in control of her life than I'd ever been. What thoughts were buried down in those black eyes?

And what about the boy? The old cliché of saving the country through saving one person . . . but clichés became so for a reason.

I found a cab willing to take me into East Jerusalem and handed him my passport to show to the guards as we drove. I closed my eyes and listened to the radio play some bizarre fusion of klezmer and a muezzin's calls.

Every ten minutes I'd open them when we arrived at another checkpoint.

- - -

The last guards were angry; the muzzles of their guns came in through the windows.

We stood outside as they searched the vehicle. The cigarette smoke and the exhaust made me grow dizzy; I leaned against a wall for balance.

"American?" asked the guard.

"Yes."

"Who are you meeting?"

"My mother. She is a tourist."

"What is her name?"

"Alexandra."

"Where is she staying?"

"In Isobel Street."

They wouldn't let the cabby through. I gave him a hundred shekels—almost all I had on me—and walked past the barbed wire.

I sat and drank one of Don Juan's cold beers from the cooler at the shop on Isobel. I could feel the day coming over me, before the radiation is turned on.

"Have you seen my friend? That little bastard Don Juan?" I grinned into the owner's face, acting drunker than I was, but not drunker than I felt.

He shook his head and smiled, and offered me another beer. I shook my head and smiled some more.

"He's a crazy kid," I offered.

He offered me the beer again. I took it and sat back down outside, feeling like the bum that I was.

There is a novel where a man journeys through a gate into a higher dimension, wherein his actions determine the fate of the universe we inhabit. That higher plane was named Yesod, another root for the word 'Mossad,' meaning "foundation." Yesod is also the Hebrew name for Eden. In Kabbalism, Yesod also represents the sexual organs (appropriate for the garden of paradise).

Mossad is thus, etymologically, a cock. Like all things, rooted in sex and violence. Fair to point out, I suppose, how it differs in this way from the Anglo-Saxon spy services, with their emphasis on "intelligence." Different "chakras" are involved! Hahaha.

But philosophy will not help me find Don Juan. Nor will this second beer. I ask the owner if I can plug in my phone, and retrace my steps to his house; over a mile away.

- - -

"Mr. Journalist!" Don Juan calls out.

"Hey, boss." I sit on his steps.

"What is it you're doing, coming to my house? You think I have beer for you? This is what you think, Palestinians just give Americans all their beer?"

"Well, since you mention it . . ."

His mother emerges.

"Bring this American a beer. He is greedy!" shouts Don Juan.

She shouts back at him and he runs into the house. She sits beside me on the steps.

"Are you staying?" she asks. "Stay, you are welcome."

The street before us is shifting in the desert light. A mirage of people, dust, stone, asphalt, and memories.

- - -

I play chess with Don Juan. I am not very good. I lose to him amicably, watching him sweep my pieces off the board.

"Why didn't she arrest you?" I ask.

"One day, one thing. Another day, something different. I'm taking your queen."

"Aren't you afraid?"

"Aren't you?"

I am holding the trident. It feels so heavy.

I awaken to the sound of helicopters. Then there's a huge noise and a soldier has a flashlight and a rifle in my face.

Another solider drags me to my feet. Don Juan's parents are standing in their nightgowns, hands on their heads.

"What in the fuck is the matter with you?" I shout at the soldiers. I get a rifle butt in my stomach. I fall to my knees. I hear Abra, Don Juan's mother, cry out. They've hit her too. The father is shouting. A soldier presses my neck to the floor with his boot. I feel a shooting pain. My breath catches in my throat.

Then a man is kneeling by me. It's David.

"Robert, how are you feeling?"

I can't even speak.

"Where is that boy, Robert?"

"I don't know."

"You've been helping him." He stands back up, out of my field of vision.

"Take them in. Burn the house," he says.

Abra is screaming. They wrap plastic cords around our wrists and haul us out into the dark, and push us into the pack of a truck. My face is on the metal and they push my legs in after me. Then they toss in Abra and Bashir. She's screaming.

18.

In the dark I can assess the trajectory of my mission. Not in any military sense; not espionage. Mission only as a missive, for every soul arrived to earth.

They bring me bread and water in the cell.

It stays dark.

19.

Sex and violence, old friends. A woman turns on a light and sits in a chair she carries in with her. I'm on the floor.

My stomach is cramping up.

"May I have some water?"

"Yes of course. There seems to have been a misunderstanding. The American embassy has someone on their way to us now. We need to know where that boy is, Robert. He's in danger. You care about him, I know. We need to find him."

She's dyed blonde, hard eyes like Rachel's but not as expressive. I say nothing and watch the movements of her face. There was an American documentary filmmaker whose genius lay in the examination of the 1970s American housewife as a heretofore unexamined insect. I adopt that perspective now, trying to piece together the logic of this woman's being as an alien might, from another world.

"Saying nothing won't help the boy. He needs both of our help."

"Won't you kill him if you find him?"

"No. We need him. Do you know where he is?"

"No." My voice is dry and raw. Where are Mr. and Mrs. Fakhoury?"

"They've been released."

"I don't believe you."

"I can't tell you any more than that. You don't mind the cell, do you? You'll be gone in an hour anyway."

She leaves and turns off the light.

In the darkness, I can see again.

19.

Love makes for strange companions; this must be one of its purposes.
To mash us together. Is violence more
heinous between intimate companions, or between strangers?

Part of me, the coward part,
wants to go home. Sit in the darkness
of my about-to-be-foreclosed-house
(so different from this darkness!) and
pretend I never left.

There is a knock on the door.

"Come in!" I shout, sarcastically.

"Robert," she says, through the
door.

I stand next to the door in the
darkness.

"Rachel."

"Are you all right?"

"Yes."

"I'll be back in an hour. If anyone
else comes before then, say nothing."

She was gone.

If there was something I could
do—anything—but there is nothing.
I'm panicking. There is always free
will, Robert, always always always.

I try to play the game I've read about for solitary confinement: throw a pebble up in the air, and then search, search, search with your fingers to find it . . .

The door opens.

Both Rachel and David stand there. I'm filled suddenly with a terrible fear that I'll be murdered.

"Come on, let's get you out of here," Rachel says, and pulls me to my feet.

- - -

We walked through long metal corridors in silence. They'd put handcuffs on me in front. Rachel said something to David in Hebrew and he responded.

They opened a door and sat me down at a table; they sat opposite.

"Robert," Rachel said. "You should go home. The American embassy wants you to go home. The Knesset wants you to go home. David here wants you to go home. Israel is too complicated for you right now."

"Actually, I'm hoping you'll stay, Robert," David said. The two of them had another rapid fire conversation in Hebrew.

"Let me show you a picture, Robert," Rachel said.

She placed a black and white photograph of a man in military uniform in front of me; a portrait.

"That's Don Juan's father," I said.

"That is Mr. Bashir Samara, photographed with two Hamas captains."

"What do you want me to do, Rachel?"

"Go. Go home. Sit in the swimming pool. Be a good American. Forget all these things too complicated for you here."

"Do you love me?" I asked her.

"We love all Americans, Robert," David said. "Come to dinner with us tonight. I'd like to talk about something with you."

"I'm afraid I don't have anything to wear," I said, holding up my handcuffs.

20.

The restaurant was a Spartan affair in Tel Aviv; totally unlike all other places I'd been in the country. It reminded me uncomfortably of home. All metal and glass.

"Do you know what this dinner is about, Robert?" she asked.

"Sure, you're recruiting me."

David laughed.

"Not a permanent job, Robert. Just to keep an eye on things for us."

Rachel said nothing.

They brought the seafood, which was delicious. Rachel devoured her sauce-soaked shrimp.

I know I am a deeply flawed man. Too often in life I've gone with the flow, following this hippy philosophy that can, in the wrong hands (mine) amount to a simple aversion to rocking the boat.

"I'll do it," I said.

21.

I am aboard an Israeli tank. It's a fun vehicle, so big. We just cruise down the streets. Like a big jet plane on an asphalt sky. I smile and wave, like a tourist. It feels horrible to do it. But I do it anyway. To try to make the irony into something that's real too.

We're in the occupied territories of the West Bank of the Jordan River. To our right is a beautiful and completely vacant city: a Palestinian city with no Palestinians. Like those Chinese cities, built for the cameras . . . a Potemkin village? Or a real one? What is the difference, when it is land?

Over the next crest is the Israeli settlement, small and brown.

The gate opens and we speed in. The Jews lift me from the tank, in their black. I am like an ancient messenger. Just as foolhardy. To go places where death is smiling wickedly into your face.

"Welcome to Kebne." The man smiles at me. He is missing an eyetooth. "I am Moshe Stancil. This is my wife, Nicole." The woman is beautiful, like a model. She does not wear a headscarf.

"Hello, hello, thanks for having me. Do you drink beer here?"

Just be an American, Robert. It's like being an idiot. The easiest thing in the world.

- - -

What world is it I am entering? This Sabbath town. Under the cruel sky of a world I no longer understand. We are dining.

Outside, the sun burns red, hotter every day.

The water of my body cool and low.

"What you must understand about Israel, Robert, is it is under our control. Whatever happens in these villages, happens everywhere."

All the megalomania in the world would not hold his absent eyetooth . .
.

"I see why you fight for it," I said. "It's beautiful. But consider the manner of your fighting. You will destroy the land you love."

"You will understand; the longer you stay with us."

I am lying under the stars, in Israel. But where is my heart?

I no longer believe I am American. But if I surrender that, what else might I be willing to change?

Nicole steps into my starlight.

"Come drink wine with us."

Where is the bushel of wheat? Well, I am it.

22.

Bushel, bushel. Bustle, bustle. I now believe Rachel wants to overthrow the Knesset, and its religious fundamentalists. But in its place, what would she put there?

Am I willing to kill for her? I fear that is what she wants.

Out of Africa I am still marching, in my dreams. I swear, Jake . . . well, what can I tell you? I seem to have left it all behind.

- - -

Israel is named for Sarah, wife of Abraham. The name means: Sarah's God. Is Sarah god herself, or is her god laughter, the laughter she is said to have laughed on discovering her pregnancy so late in life. Like all gods, Israel's is one of pregnancy.

But the question is: who is she giving birth to? Boy or girl. What tongue shall the child speak. And what words, will he, or she, say.

Jews were born in the Iron Age, around 600 B.C., the written Torah the merging of two oral Canaanite traditions: two compelling fictions, one of Abraham the Founding Father, and one of Moses. Each acknowledging in kind the earlier empires which preceded it: Egypt, and Mesopotamia.

The Palestinians are equally ancient. They are recorded in hieroglyphics as the Palestu, their ancient city of Gaza likely linked to Giza by trade.

To some degree understanding the conflict of the Middle East is no more complicated than the conflict between men and women. Gods and goddesses.

Love, and its mutual dances, keeping the right degree of shadows over our loving bowers, trembling, before one another's eyes.

\- - -

Take me, and foul the rest, for I will play David, and Joseph both, sent into empire to destroy it. Take me, character, fit into the rest, for the message to all our people, of revolution:

23.

The Palestinians hold a funeral near the village and the Jews are firing over their heads.

The Torah records in exquisite detail the ancient belief in the magical power of language, a magic expressed chiefly through fantastically ornate curses. I open my mouth; I start shouting as I run towards the funeral party.

Nicole and Moshe shout after me; the Jews stop firing. None of my words can be heard over the helicopter gunships sent in, hovering. One of the Palestinian women's headscarf blows off and she stoops to retrieve it. She looks at me with beautiful eyes.

I watch them pass, walking down towards the cemetery below the hill.

The gunships follow them for a moment and I raise my fists and shout at them. One of the gunners waves at me, smiling.

- - -

The aborigines of Australia—and many Native American tribes—

believed waking life is a dream we awaken from in sleep. This makes more sense to me in Israel, a place where even prayers are forbidden by law in certain places, an acknowledgment by the (ostensibly) secular state of Israel that spirits exist, and can be raised.

I say nothing to my hosts and go to my tiny room and lie on the bed, closing my eyes in the heat.

Nicole comes to the door and says "Robert?" but I do not open my eyes.

Outside I can hear the gunships moving away. Some men are still shouting.

The funeral was for a boy.

- -

"What are you doing here?" I asked Nicole.

"Surviving."

24.

I spend my days walking outside the compound, which security does not like. I call Rachel.

"How is Don Juan's family?" I ask.

"I don't know."

"Well find out."

"I'm coming to visit you."

"Going to arrest me again?"

"Not this time."

Love is terrible because of its size. Its dimensionless direction. The sea within, subject to tides, by one thousand moons, interlocking orbits, and plunging all the while on another gravitational curve, down, and down, and down:

It would be better if this were only a love story, and I could redeem myself by being a good lover, and by knowing the right things to say — or, absent that — if I could be simpler.

The helicopters hover over at night while she is in my bed.

She too is a gunship, cut from this old stone, like the monuments the Canaanites erected to determine the boundaries of their plots: "this far and no further" her body says, writ under my skin.

God is love, the Christians say; but I never agree during the act of love. What God would murder our personalities in this way, cutting us into stone?

25.
I am getting married.

26.

This record is of an American man, but I am no longer American. Its pretense, as that in all fiction, is that people remain similar enough over the course of time to be tracked: to know that this character, Robert, is similar enough to the Robert you met at the beginning to judge and learn from his actions and the events Robert took part in.

So I must lie now a bit more, to continue to be the Robert I was—at least for a little while—to continue this story. Because as an Israeli, I would never write any of this down.

27.

The rubble of Gaza is like the moon. A colonized moon, with dozens of children scrambling over every surface.

I am a new employee in an NGO that Rachel, my new wife, recommended.

I stand and deliver water and grain.

I have not seen Don Juan or his family since the arrest. Rachel is on a mission and will not answer her phone.

I am afraid for her. And for these people.

What does it mean, that the same people should kill and then befriend those they've murdered? Alternately embracing and stabbing their beloved? Is it their insane God, inscribed in their Torah? Is it, as politicians say, merely the effects of climate change?

We too are an effect of climate change: the human race.

They queue in the dust and take the supplies back to their encampments, where they are rebuilding. The NGO is registered in Washington, DC but it is Israeli money, so Rachel assures me. How can I tell? The water is real.

I can't see what I am to do yet. But that's wrong too: I am already doing it.

Why did she marry me?

28.

According to the orthodox and conservative Jews, I am not a Jew. But to the reform Jews, I am. I suppose that makes me one third Jew.

I do not observe Passover. I will not hide from the evil gods of this region. I aim to kill them.

29.

My report on the Orthodox settlement I filed in David's office. Like the United States espionage apparatus, much of Mossad's energy is spent observing their own people. I am now an informer for the secret police.

Mossad means the generative organs, that center chakra. The fount of paradise. The means of the survival of the species. Who I am now must be seen through that lens: this mercury, around the slow sun of the genitals of the Jews. These Jewish genitals, of all colors, scrabbled furiously into the earth, whispering in a language I cannot yet speak.

But that is not enough. Part of me is American enough to remember why I came. To claim the woman, and my story.

- - -

I stand in the shattered mosque, looking for Don Juan. Thousands of bodies moving in their prayers.

"I've seen your man," a man said beside me.

"Yes?"

"Follow me."

There have been no Israeli rockets this week. The Knesset's phone app designed to warn civilians of incoming strikes does not always work, and I have picked more than one tiny shard of cement out of my shins from the blasts.

We duck through a devastated apartment building and move towards the ocean, that ocean from which the Palestinians are said to have come, from Crete, so many thousands of years ago.

I see him then standing in the alleyway. He is indeed a man now. Only 14 years old. But old enough, in the Jewish tradition.

"Don Juan!"

He grins.

30.

We move through the devastated land down towards the ocean. I say nothing. The man and Don Juan are talking in Arabic. They say the Israelis are going to attack again—only a matter of time. But despite the morass of exploded concrete and twisted steel, the thought of war seems impossible here. The sea is the only real thing, and the light.

When will I be forgiven for all I have done? And for all I am still to do? And is forgiveness necessary?

"We need your help, Robert," Don Juan says.

"Tell me."

- - -

I am learning to fire a gun.

"You won't need it unless everything goes wrong. But when it does, you'll have it."

Me with my glasses. I can't hit anything further than twenty yards. But at ten, I can.

Loyalty stems from the Latin *lex*, in turn from the Greek *legein*, "to say." So loyalty is a product of speech. The more you speak to people, the more loyal you are to them.

That is how it is with me. In some ways, spying is impossible. You are bound to be loyal to your companions, whoever they are. Of whatever language. Of whatever humor. Whatever religion. Whatever nation. But what is the quantity of speech required to earn loyalty? What law and *lex* can abide with thee, after which words in what amounts, binding you to the divine spirit of that long avenue through time and people and history, I don't know: but I will find out. Perhaps like everything, it is a decision. A decision to listen. Will these words be the ones? Or these. Or these. Or these words, now:

31.

I carry the gun next to my chest under my shirt. The Israeli officer is manning a checkpoint beneath the severed overpass at the eastern edge of Gaza.

He is alone. I show him my American passport.

"Where in America are you from?"

"Los Angeles," I say, and I take out the gun.

What is it, Robert, what did I do? What door is this one?

Death works these strange wonders, no less so with me. I can say it was for Rachel. Let it be that. We'll blame the woman; easier that way. A Mossad woman, moved to remove her own house . . . but the truth is something else. Americans rooting for the underdog.

He smiled for some reason. And so did I, when I shot him.

- - -

Whatever else, at least I've chosen a side. But it is a side which does not yet exist.

32.

The muezzin is crying and I enter the mosque, standing at the entrance. The flood of people. I know this Islamic practice is from that old wonder under Gobekli Tepe, Potbelly Hill, in Turkey . . . the expression of our ancestors' ancient bemusement, horror and fascination with our sheer growing numbers, for the Middle East is the middle. All roads may lead to Rome, but they pass through here.

Rumi says love is a wasteland, and so too for Palestine. The people are huddled under the concrete and under the barrier of their god, both imaginary, both bright and careful and solemn, the human profundity of their presence in the casual expression of their movements, the calm neighborly regard, for that too is holy, as Ginsberg says, everything. Everything.

I'm crying and return to my hotel to sleep.

When I awaken, David is sitting by my bed, like the Biblical character, looking to see what we shall write next onto the wall of the king.

33.

So many men with guns have laid claim to the children of their patrol; I'm told it was so with the one I killed, too. He didn't look like a child rapist, but how can you tell? And in truth I would have done it simply because Don Juan asked.

In part it is because I want to betray my own country, and it seems easier to do it here, where Americans are still seen as casual interlopers, curious bystanders. At home it would still be too painful.

"The Knesset wishes to meet you," David says, and I go with him.

- - -

"Knesset" means "gathering." In English, "gather" is closely related to "good," from the Proto-Indo-European root *-ghedh*. For the greater good. Unite as one, with or without a king, in common purpose, to defeat evil. Or to commit it. Or both . . .

"What brought you to Israel, Robert?" asks Minister Atid.

"A woman."

"Are you Jewish?"

"No, I'm not. Well, an aspiring Jew."

"I heard you have married."

"Yes."

"It was a Jewish ceremony?"

"Yes."

"Congratulations. Do you believe, Robert, that Israel occupies a special place in history?"

His beard is quite beautiful. His eyes, less so. The minister's eyes are like an old and malevolent turtle, plotting his final range of tricks.

"I am an American citizen and so of course I benefit from the relationship between our two nations. I am not a religious man."

"But I want to know: are we special?"

"All places are special. And all people. Israel has plenty of problems; so does America. I think there are worse places. I think you are still learning."

"Yes, of course! Jews love to learn! And we are leaning a great deal. Ha ha ha! Robert, you were recommended to us as a trustworthy man. Is it your desire to become a citizen of Israel?"

"Yes."

"Under the Reform doctrine you can, of course. Under others, less easily. Are you circumcised?"

"Yes."

"That part is easy, then. But you are not religious. That is harder now. To ignore the Torah. Have you studied it?"

"Yes, some."

"That's good. What I want to ask you is this: imagine that my wife is sick. I come to you, demanding your advice. You are not a doctor, but I come to you as a friend, and I ask: what is God doing to me, to make my wife sick?"

"It sounds like a question for a rabbi."

"You talk a bit like a rabbi. Israel is a woman, Robert. And she is ill. But what I want to understand is: how did this come to be? And what am I, a minister of this state, to do about it?"

His face is like a minefield that has been partially detonated. His voice is strong but his body is weak; his hands tremble.

"You must do as you see fit, minister. That is what you were elected to do."

"Elected, yes. I know. Will you help me?"

"If I can."

"There is an American man, visiting here. He represents a certain mining firm. Our friends suggested to me that you would be the perfect person to meet him. I'm told you are already acquainted with him. Will you meet this man, for me?"

"Who is he?"

"Mr. Joshua Brewston."

This heaviness in my head. The weight is memory, but also purpose. Once it weighs enough, it will bend my eyes to their task, and my hands, and legs.

"The man is an asshole," I say.

Minister Atid laughed, like a mad Santa Claus, dressed in black.

34.

Over the dry land, I can hear my breath. I whistle while I drive. Sarah's God is, in addition to one of fertility, also its opposite. Death. Dryness. Desert. In the wilderness everything is visible; each man, each house, each tree takes on the distinct outlines of god, which only means: in the desert, you truly become acquainted with the world.

I pull up by a temporary office trailer that looks like it could come from any dusty mining town in America.

I knock on the aluminum door.

Josh is a salesman. Prices are so good in wartime.

Can you kill all the evil men, Robert? And wouldn't you then be an evil man?

"Robert," he says, and shakes my hand. "Why don't you come in?"

- - -

Corporate energies. Like an old suit, now a little tight around the gut.

"How is business?"

"Business is good. The Knesset sent you? How did you get so politically connected, Robert? Ha ha ha."

"I married well."

"Ha ha ha. What can I do for you?"

I have the reverse experience to claustrophobia, being with an American—our predisposition for open spaces and limitless distance hovers over my body—

"Are you all right?"

"You have some water?" I sat in the one of the spinning office chairs.

"Here."

The best thing to do would be to beat him with my fists until I can't beat him anymore. Who are you working for, Robert? The future. Work for the future, Robert.

"Leave Israel. Or I'll kill you."

"You feeling all right, Robert? You want me to call a doctor?"

"You heard what I said?"

"Yeah I heard. What's this about?"

I stand and lurch to the door. "You're a warmonger, Josh."

I get in my car and drive.

With the support of a government, you become an arm of that government. But what if part of your actions are aimed to dismantle said government? The metaphor is not right. A government is not a body, but a direction. And all the bodies' small gravity wells, trying to pull the lever, to drop the planet down the hatch, and tug it north, south, east and west, spinward and coreward . . .

I call Rachel, but she does not answer. I send her a text: *where is Don Juan?*

35.

If you can dip into life--into a woman--into the right mandate for your transformation-if you can re-form-make ends meet, not financially, and not in the genetic code, but in the body anyway, in sex, but also in the mind:

Bend into life, dip in and wait for the name of the feeling, each one different, discordant and secular and holy, bright and bold.

I am bright and bold but I have forgotten: and so has she, each time.

She is crying, in what sounds like pleasure.

It is pleasure.

I thought she was the dark one but perhaps it is me. The murder in me is like a rich fluid, like semen, a vital fluid that contains information about who I am: more than information, of course, a seed.

Murder is a seed, growing in me, here in the Middle East.

If the act of love is also an attack—and all attacks are born from love—perhaps this is also the nature of Mossad, its genital origin, seeds of plants and animals in our gardens, surrounding us . . .

She is my garden, but she is movement, around my body, her warm skin and her dark hair the shelter from forces I can't yet understand.

"Where is Don Juan?"

But she says nothing, breathing against me like a fossil which is alive.

36.

Joshua Brewston has flown home to the United States. Minister Atid called to congratulate me on my work.

Israel is different to me now. Israel, Palestine; Palestine, Israel. The Levant, land of the rising sun. Land of the Canaanites. Canaan may mean "Land of the subjugated" or "Land of the purple" (referring to the royal purple made from murex shells, native to the region). Indeed, the purple would be a good reason to subjugate the region. And, with brief interregnums, the region has always been ruled by someone else. Always a vassal state.

Am I to perpetuate this history, and cooperate in the suppression of its people, both Jews and Palestinians? No. But it seems as though I already have . . .

Power is such a terrible evil; such a profound magic spell. Only exercise it, and you understand at once its fascination: "might make right" is wrong, but it is *close* to being right, because action makes its own reality. Impose your will and learn its freedoms . . .

I drink coffee all day and sit in the hotel café in the heat. Perhaps I will die here. In some ways, I am already dead. The new me is being born, inside.

Rachel and I are to buy a house. With the cooperation of the Israeli government.

I find there is a smile on my face.

37.

It is the lead weight; I see that now. Each wall, each tree of fruit, I see that. This garden of Mossad's. Of Eden's. No different than the problems of success generally: now, Adam, you have tamed through your god this plain of earth. You have subdued the creatures of the field. Named reality, with your mouth. Yes, you are like god.

The loneliness of the top. The same lethargy and sociopathy that infects the rich (affluenza . . . ha ha ha) affects all humanity to some degree: we the victors. We the overlords. The weight of victory is itself death.

I want a son. I make love to my wife furiously, focused on that instant of conception. I am not entirely well. I read books on male fertility and go jogging incessantly in the early morning and evenings when it is cool.

I am learning Hebrew. I have learned our new neighbors' names, many of them government agents, to keep us safe.

The lead weight, its noose and yoke of the finest silver, extends over my shoulders and into my mouth, like a sheath around my sword . . . lifting me up, lifting . . .

But not yet.

- - -

There's a knock at the door. My wife is already in the closet, like a shadow, loading her shotgun.

I open the front door.

"May I come in?" he says.

"Who are you?"

"I work for American intelligence. My name is Mainz."

"Come in."

My wife is standing in the entryway, shotgun in hand. The man tips an invisible cap to her. I shut the door behind him.

"You're an interesting couple," he says.

"Would you like tea, Mr. Mainz?" Rachel says.

"I've come to warn you," he says. His face is like a thousand Harvard graduates: well-meaning, pale, earnest, frivolous even, polished and naïve. Like my former country. And armed. Armed with so many weapons.

"You have made unfortunate enemies. Josh Brewston for one, but he's nothing. But the board of directors of his company is upset that their mining concern was not speedily arranged through the Knesset. He blames you."

"Why are you telling us?" asks Rachel.

"We share an employer," Mainz says. "The people of Palestine."

"I'll make tea," Rachel says.

"No, don't. I must go. Be careful, hey?"

He let himself out. Rachel switched the safety on the shotgun and put it back in the closet.

I looked out the window where Mainz was getting into his car. I could see him, illuminated by the instrument panel. He was speaking into his phone, and looking back at my house, a haunted look on his face.

38.

Killing is always a mistake. I know that now. But it is the kind of mistake which invites others.

I am on a plane. Returning to America.

Inside the belly of the plane, I can sleep. Outside, the Earth is still the same. Ceaseless change, and the colors of the sky, moving west, young man: tell me, who are you now? Not so young man. The flight attendant moves in some distant universe. I feel drunk, though I'm not.

I am selling my property in California.

Whatever happens to me now will happen in the Old World. As though we really ever left it. All worlds are new and old, in whatever hemisphere.

- - -

The real estate agent is happy to sign me; she claims it is a seller's market.

The bar is so quiet; it is Tuesday. And the light of Los Angeles so like Israel's. Jerusalem is 31 degrees

North; LA is 34, about 200 miles apart.

Someone is knocking on the door to the bar, a drunk. The door is open, but he keeps knocking. I go over and open it for him and stumbles in.

What is this feeling? Not the light—not only that. Not only the decision to leave, like all of my decisions, romantically pure, and taken with a degree too much haste...

No, it is the moment itself, the flow of time in this moment. Its slowness. That is what I crave. LA is a slow city, despite being a metropolis, but not as slow as Jerusalem. The religious flow of time, river never the same twice, but always around your legs.

"Give me another please."

I want to see my city drunk before I leave.

It isn't only the woman. It is the boy. Which is first? I don't know.

I serve them both.

39.

I understand now the love affair between the United States and Israel. It has nothing to do with religion. And everything to do with violence.

Violence comes from the Latin *violare*, from the Proto-Indo-European root *–weie* "to go after with vigor or desire." Related to "gain."

After all, it is through violence that we obtain food. That we achieve mastery over our destiny. That we learn.

Yet I do not understand violence. How can one understand it? Is it by nature beyond comprehension?

I fly back to my new home, Israel.

Now I am part of the problem. Now part of the solution. One more variable in an increasingly complex equation.

Rachel is standing in the kitchen, in her underwear.

I lean against the cabinets and look at her. She kisses my cheek and presses herself against me.

One day, I will be free. But not in this life.

Outside the muezzin is calling. I want to sing with him.

- - -

Set out no more. What is come is now I can do nothing to betray. Sink fast and die low, inside this undertow, sweeping me away, under the dead sea.

I shall have to destroy the temple again.

This fire inside, what is it? I want to give it a name. This lull, this lilt. Tilt me, against your skin, and take me, into what you promise.

The human body is writ with all these experiences, waiting to be unpacked. A million code words and passages, as temples themselves.

It worked twice. Third time is the charm.

40.

I will need to learn something about explosives.

41.

The Wailing Wall, western wall of the second Jewish temple destroyed by the Romans, is approximately half a kilometer in length. At its peak height, the wall is 32 meters tall, a quarter of which is underground. The stone is limestone, called *meleke*, "kingly stone."

Samson knew the power of temples. Destroy the building, and some of the spirit leaves with it.

I am fortunate that Mossad also wants it to be killed. Adherents set against their own church.

42.

The explosion is light and meaning at once: no ruins but within. Now we are building, at last, inside.

The noise is immense; David, Rachel and I watch through our glasses. Now we must arrest the Orthodox; they will be insane.

- - -

Orthodox, upright honor, upright honor, your honor, be upstanding, be upright, be right, and up:

We herd them into the wagons.

- - -

Wail, from *wa!*, woe in many languages.

Disinterring sadness, so it may rest awhile, in the bodies of men, and not always just in one grave. We can always build another temple. But there is only one year like this.

Rachel is frightened. I sing camp songs to draw the ire of the men, as we ride to the prison.

For their own protection; lest they hurt themselves or others, here in the destruction of their most sacred relic at the hands of their own henchmen.

Or my henchmen. Who is working for whom? We are obeying some other spell, from within . . .

\- - -

News broadcasts already exploding; and the Cyclopean conspiracy theories of the Middle East weaving a new tapestry, brightly colored, but there is relief, too. We can all feel it. Even the Orthodox.

As when a dearly beloved relative, suffering terribly for many, many years, finally dies.

43.

The Wailing Wall is no more.

It has been said, by some men, that it is ruins the universe wants, that the work of men is merely to produce ruins, so that the gods can admire our handiwork after we are gone.

I know this is not true. So does David. My new friend David. My brother.

We brothers know the Wall is only one wall. And any great wall of however a storied history must too be ruins, and we will celebrate it.

Ruins from ruins; death from death; and then life.

What else would there be, from ruins.

I kiss her under the huge sky.

I am happy.

44.

We leave the country for our own protection. I suggest Poland. She finds it a strange enough suggestion to say yes. We are off to Krakow. I didn't even bring a jacket; I'll have to buy one there.

\- - -

There's this feeling I can't shake. Like there's a small delinquent well of anti-gravity hanging around two to three inches around my body. It feels like a blessing.

We joke that this is our honeymoon, and it does feel like it. The snow is beautiful; I've bought a fur lined trenchcoat so I look like a spy from Conrad's novel, 100 years gone.

Here, Rachel's darkness is almost defeated by the northern light; but not quite. There is a legend that a dragon founded Krakow and sleeps beneath it. We go to the dragon's cave and slip away from the tourists, kissing Cro-Magnons in the phosphorescent light.

God is so malleable, in the end, but stories less so. You can blow up the dragon's cave, but the dragon remains, even in death . . .

I've taken up smoking again and do it in the hotel bed, watching her dark eyes.

45.

Parks and cafés and buses, street-cars and museums, restaurants, bars, shops minarets mosques temples street corners, bedrooms dining rooms hallways offices board rooms arcades opium dens churches and the Knesset, shut down in strange relief, wanton relief, even the Orthodox, set now in a strange relief, though it is within.

Calls for Jewish versions of jihad are heard, of course, killing all infidels in a thousand mile radius, rebuild the third temple at once, blow up the Dome of the Rock, the Hagia Sophia, lay waste to Palestine, and Egypt, all the usual profanities, but behind it a curious lack of energy, with the small god gone, after so many centuries, it is relief. Like leaving college. Leaving home. Your first international flight. Your first love. First lovemaking. First job.

First detonation of the Wailing Wall (and there would be others). A season spited but well-maintained. The circumcised cocks and generous pudenda of Mossad, the garden of Eden in the center chakra, more relaxed than they have ever been, and ever more watchful because of it.

I too am now Mossad, though my Hebrew is poor at best. I am learning.

The crater is being built into a public square, the Knesset announces. This too with a strange lack of force. Like announcing a new freeway offramp. Like celebrating a lunar eclipse. Excited, and calm, with a coffee in hand, and the stars shining above.

- - -

Jew comes from Judah; it means "celebrated." Celebrate may be related to "celerity" in the sense of "swift." Jews swift in the dancing, and in the setting down to tea, in the square at dawn, on all days, under whatever ruinous or magnificent moon, blue red or white, yellow brown or black, celebrated, and celebrated swift and right all . . .

Righteous celebrations.

Or so I see it now, before what came.

Part 2
War

46.

The original meaning of war, in the Proto-Indo-European, *wers*, was "to bring into confusion." In turn, "confuse" means at root "to mix together." Love and war being profound mixtures.

Depending how one counts them, the state of Israel has been involved from 1948 to the present in 34 wars and military actions.

And, depending on how one counts, the United States has been involved in 22 over that same period.

Comparatively, over the first 68 years of the United States' history (again, subject to debate), the United States was involved in 19 wars.

Truth is the first casualty in war, wrote Philip Snowden in 1916. It may be this betrays an old fashioned unitary view of the truth. I am not certain we can still lay claim to such universals, here a century later. It may be that truth is instead revealed in war, in all its multiform glory and horror. The truth is, after all, confusing.

- - -

I sit and wait, though I am not very good with the rifle. In the silence, I am thinking of a documentary I saw.

Then I see them moving.

I fire twice and the soldier dies.

They are moving towards the building.

Sasha is screaming.

I climb the ladder and she is firing, then climbing. I duck into the hatch and fire below with my handgun, but there are more of them.

A grenade, and then I climb after her, to the roof.

The documentary was chimpanzees. They do border patrol in platoons. Sitting by the side of the culvert, watching together. For the movement of the enemy.

There is a drain, mostly blown to pieces, but the anchor bolts still appear to adhere to the concrete. I urge

Sasha to climb down them; she is lighter than me.

The sun is so bright.

She makes it down and I follow.

One of the Israeli soldiers sights me and fires. The bullet enters my left calf muscle and I limp around the corner, down to the tunnels.

Tunnels are our oldest friends. Like gravity. Perhaps gravity is, too, a tunnel.

We scuttle along, our rats, along with a couple of real rats, back to the depot.

Rag tied over my leg.

Pain is a friend too. Or frenemy, anyway. Like the bazooka that blows up in your face. Or the lover that cheats on you, but fucks you better for it. The leering regard of the station agent, sent to wool too long, waiting for something that might never come.

We are coming, but I'm growing old. And information sharing, always so strange to me, the way people know things (it must be psychic radiation! ha ha), now grows ever faster.

Mossad cannot protect me. But then, it's not clear anyone can protect Mossad either.

What are we fighting for?

Everyone has a reason. That's one of the crazier things about it. Everyone has one, though they don't always express it. Is the trick to remember that the reason is not the war itself? There was a reason before the war that began it. These things are true. The *casus belli*, of whatever kind; but that is not the reason that sustains war. That is something else. Yes, like love. Futile love. Love unconquerable.

I pour water over the wound while Sasha uses the last of the heroin on me. I wish I were a stronger man and could just dig the bullet out with a knife between my teeth. Maybe I will be that man one day.

I lean back while she does the work. Under the quality of the drug, the tunnel depot is a small god. Household Roman god. River god of the under stones. Apes crawling to victory and damnation.

- - -

I have been reassigned to office work, which I do not like. I need time to heal. In these kinds of wars, you are a solider one day and a civilian the next. With no uniforms, the easiest way to tell combatants from non-combatants is whether they're holding a gun.

But now everyone holds a gun. But not me; not today. Today I am writing. Journalist again. Journal, the daily happenings, of this medieval city, Jerusalem, a city whose name means "foundation of peace." What a laugh that is.

The newspaper is *The Daily Clairvoyant*. We make predictions. Estimate tendencies. We are an intelligence service, but a public one. So too with all newspapers, of course. Some more intelligent than others.

We are loath to use artillery; so many priceless relics in the old city. Never know what you might blow up. And it could be a hospital. Of course, wars do like blowing those up too. We may even have done it, like the Israelis did in Gaza; I am not sure.

Street fighting is a real neighborhood event. Like family feuds in Tennessee. Apes screaming in the trees, at the injustice of the world.

Running. Running with Don Juan. Don Juan, save me from this long equilibrium, rough me up, use me, take me into this night, under your stars, and I will follow you into Europe, and into Africa.

I will, and I will. Run.

Run.

We're moving into the border country with Egypt, towards the tunnels. Going to Cairo.

There was no Moses, but the Sinai has seen a lot of motherfuckers over the years. How many? How many Moseses flew through the blasted land wondering what strange gods moved through their bodies over the course of their surrender to the elements, over the course of their education.

The boy Don Juan is a man, and I am a boy. Educate means "lead out."

Into the wilderness. Rachel is in Germany raising money. Sasha is in hiding.

Don Juan, who I think of now as Lord Byron's Don Juan, a character Byron forced to be pronounced "Joo-un" (to fit his meter; ha!), has taken me under, out of the starlight, into this crowd of immigrants under the tunnels under Gaza, a Palestinian bride, a man moving a new washing machine, militants with RPGs, men, women and children moving quietly and speedily under the dark of the border into Egypt.

Lord Byron died in the Greek revolution in 1820. But I and Don Juan will not die.

I won't let it happen.

47.

Bombing. Bombing is thunder. There is no delight in it as there is in Sasha. She tastes like seawater.

\- - -

We await the end in the dim light. We may not be able to dig our way out the door.

\- - -

The Sinai has no cedars left in it.

\- - -

We are moving towards Cairo on foot. World War Three, of a kind. But we knew that already. We do have water, but no food. My telephone does not have any juice.

Cairo is two hundred klicks west. We are holding out our thumbs. Who knows who could pick us up. Government troops. Jihadis. American businessmen. Mercenaries. Maybe the last dozen Yemeni Jews, still clutching their ancient jeweled daggers, will invite us aboard for luck on the riding deck of one of their traveling circusmobiles as in Afghanistan, covered in bright jingling treasures every square centimeter . . .

Sasha is a beautiful woman, but in war all women are beautiful. Starry eyed damsels of the revenants of our ancestors, ghosts still abjuring us to work not yet done, not yet deceased, lingering, in their arms, their hair, and their cries, to the sky, men are only incidental in this league-driven travesty, my own, and all of ours, on the earth:

"Is your phone still out?"

"It hasn't magically recharged itself in the absence of solar panels, no."

"I think I smell water."

"Your nose is better than mine. Which direction?"

"There."

Sinai is named for Sin. She was the moon goddess of Sumer, and later the Akkadians, and Arabs. I can't prove it, but likely the Proto-Indo-

European "sin" is linked to it too. Do we not always blame women when things go wrong? And their moon.

A fighter jet has flown over us. I think an Egyptian one.

Cairo means "place of combat," referring to the ancient battle between Seth and Horus that took place there. Horus, "the high-flying one," hawk-headed god, was the son of Isis and Osiris. Seth is the god of the desert. Horus is, in many ways, Egypt — its first national god. So the battle that gives Cairo its name can be understood as the city's battle to survive against the desert.

But the battle is also a racial one: Seth is identified with Nubia, and so the battle is also an ongoing one of white supremacy.

The black desert and its sun versus the white city and its water. Empires have certainly been built from less.

Sinai contains eight chief oases.

We have been fortunate and hitched a ride with date traders. We have been given guest dates. The finest dessert anywhere. Sasha chews them with relish, winking at me.

The oasis is Wadi al Hummur, at Qesm Abu Rdis, on the coast of the Gulf of Suez. 120 klicks southeast of Cairo.

At the oasis some Arabs greet us and invite us to dinner. Of course we accept. They even allow me to plug my phone into their solar generator.

I am a killer in the desert. It feels good.

48.

In Cairo we are shuttered below the tea room, out of sight. Egypt is not unsympathetic to our revolution, but we'd make for a tidy reward to certain parties…

What are the stories of revolution? Well, these tunnels, aren't they. Like the barricades of Paris. Heading in, and it's a one way trip. Wait for the light: another dimension, on the other side.

We gorge ourselves on aish and baba ghanoush. Sasha smokes cigarettes and I stare at my phone. No new messages.

The tricky thing about modern war is: who do you kill? What, exactly, do you blow up?

One thing I do know is: Israel will no longer be a Jewish state. Any more than America is a white state.

Who are the chief opponents to our aims?

And what exactly are the sympathies of the army?

Easy to say: eliminate your enemies, and their supporters. But even if one waves one's invisible magic wand and they vanish from this earth, the results are still undesirable.

Will a multi-ethnic state be democratic? Even republican? Do the people know what they want?

I take one of her cigarettes and smoke it. Waiting is the worst.

\- - -

Place of combat in my dreams, from the sounds of the street. Why should I love these cities so? What is the light telling me?

There is a knock at the door. I open it; it is David.

"Come with me," he says.

And I do.

49.

The logic of bombing is the same as the logic of war, or a bad love affair. You think, at the beginning: I won't do that. How absurd.

You see the woman manipulating you; it's ridiculous. Why would she think she can get away with something like that?

Why would she think I'm such a simple man, to fall for her tricks.

Why would she think I would remember. Or forget. Why would she think I would love her more, for her tricks.

Why would she. Why would I give the order, for the plane, to come over Jerusalem.

Bombing is not good politics. It's horrendous politics. Just mass murder. Wanton destruction. The word is from the Greek, *bombos*, a deep and hollow sound. Like a bell. Hells' bells, righteous and unafraid, unleashed uselessly against the people of Jerusalem, in a holy fire, without reward, without justification, and without even memory, if you like, for the memory of the moments before can be erased in the blast. Perhaps that is one of the purposes of bombs. They are a kind of time machine. They suck you forward, into the future:

The Israelis are no better than the Palestinians when it comes to the placement of military installations. After all, it's a densely populated region. And, after all, you want those soldiers nearby, where they can be of use. Right near all those schools and hospitals. Right near all those middle class houses. Near the ghettoes and the alleys.

In some respects, perhaps, short of nuclear blasts which we have agreed we will not use, for fear of the IDF's own nuclear arsenal, Jerusalem can hardly be bothered by bombing. It has survived it before. It is part of the texture of their reality, like white yellow stone. Like date palms.

I am targeting, from the Mediterranean. In our ship waving a flag of New Guinea. One hundred nautical miles off the coast of the Levant.

50.

What does Sarah's God want? This god of pregnancy in the middle of the desert. If we can understand that, perhaps we can understand this unending war in the Middle East. This horrifying, laughing God. This God of Jerusalem.

I believe it is more than mere hunger. Though of course the god of Abraham can be understood as a drooling psychopathic Lear, pulling down his own house, I believe there is a less violent logic parallel to it. We can say it is simply another logic of Lear's personality, the aging white patriarch. From love, and the wintering of his desires, comes that perpetual desire in kings to leave his mark on the world.

Remember me, says Jerusalem. Oh please, remember me.

We remember you so well. So well it is like a second reality. Parallel to this one. Neither dream nor waking but virtual, a video game one cannot stop playing. A book one is unable to put down.

Sarah's God is one of memory, and the failures of memory. What never happened can be made to have happened. And what is happening can be made to be forgotten.

The lights of the targeting systems play over Rachel's face in the command center of the belly of the ship, and I am reading Zamyatin.

51.

Of course revolution is eternal recurrence. Arrive again, and know yourself. Howth Castle and Environs, Joyce's old Irish chestnut, or wherever it is you're fond of, some hill or bend in the stream, a shadow of some bushes, and the animal you saw there: it can happen again!

We'll help it happen again. In lightning.

\- - -

Even the arrow from the bow achieves relativistic speeds, did you know? This is why it is able to penetrate the tree trunk. Because it is moving more slowly through time as it picks up speed . . . killing from a distance is also a tunnel. But it's not one I want to see the other side of . . .

\- -

"We have to dive! Dive! We've been here too long!"

Rachel shouts into her phone until it stops working. Someone is firing on us, as we sink into the water.

"Who is it?" I ask.

"The Americans!" Her pale face is like a painting. I am her conscience; but consciences aren't much use when running. Only when deciding who to kill. I try to sleep through the depth charges, but the sounds of them are demons. Reaching into my head to colonize the gray matter . . .

- - -

It is an Israeli submarine of German manufacture. Instructions on how to close the hatches are in Hebrew, English, and High German. The word Hebrew appears to stem from an ancient word for "immigrant" – literally, the word means "the other side of the river Euphrates." According to legend, Abraham fled Mesopotamia for Palestine to marry his sister Sarah. However many waves of immigrants actually comprised the movement of Canaanites to Palestine we don't know; but the Torah is ultimately a revised Gilgamesh, the national epic of Mesopotamia. Stories, though they lie, are wonderful at revealing these cutting truths, like the blasts from the Americans above us.

It is rather unpleasant to suddenly be at war with the United States and Israel at once. But I suppose this is what I wanted. Or, anyway, what I signed up for . . .

The woman is a serpent (after all, it's what Eve's name meant . . . ha!), yelling at the men and turning valves madly about. I help with what I can, which isn't much. Her face is alive with the music of violence.

"Get over here and lean against this wall!"

I do as she tells me. The sub is small; it's the two of us and five men. All Mossad. This strange Jewish dick, bent curiously into the wind, pursuing a pussy previously unknown, and likely undocumented in human history—will it mean the end of the Jews as we know them? Whatever Mossad's end is it ain't endogamous . . .

We are surfacing north of the Bosphorus, having slipped through undetected. We cycle the air and then slip back down in the night, towards Odessa.

52.

And now what shall you know, my dark friend? Shall you know how it was for me? In that interminable history. All history is romance. This terrible news sweeps over me, but I am only a man, and small. Tell me your news, instead, so I might keep to it, and forget:

- - -

Odessa is ten thousand streets like I have never seen. A lyre of the north.

The tobacco here is delicious. But the people frighten me.

Rachel and I get high on opium. I hold her against me in the dark. Somewhere, I am flying. It is not here. I am flying over Berkeley California, to visit Michael Chabon. Hello, Michael. Michael, it's me. What are you doing down there, you silly man? Are you still swearing at Joyce? Come, hold my hand. Fly with me.

Fly with me, Peter Pan. Into the night.

- - -

These waters are delicious. Like the waters of Greece. You can feel too much, I think. Or maybe not. But I feel more now. The drug of war. Or is it only life? Is life war? Something more, of course. She is swimming.

David is here. Shouting something. I feel I will die. From this feeling. It is so delicious. Of the beauty of the Odessa night.

She is swimming in the water by the submarine. Nothing can surprise Odessa. Not submarines. Not mermaids. Certainly not bearded Americans. They are beyond surprise. Into a territory of their own.

David is shouting in my ear, but I cannot hear him. I am out in space.

"They're coming! They're coming."

The Americans are coming.

Down the street. With their shaved faces. And their uniforms. And their berets. Their jeweled vests. The Romans are coming to arrest the Jews.

- - -

The submarine sinks under the sea, after David slips down the hatch. Rachel climbs out of the water. The Americans put the handcuffs around my wrists. Rachel slaps the sergeant's face. Her they don't handcuff. They tug us down the quay, towards the unmarked Jeep.

"Where are you taking us?" I ask.

"You're American?"

"I used to be."

53.
Lead me, Rachel, I am your fire in the night. Burning.

54.

She is asleep on the cot in the dark. They've put us in the same cell. A strangely humane gesture.

The night is beautiful inside—this night inside me. I feel I could do anything in it. Have done anything in it. Whatever else, at least I have left my old world behind, to retreat to the Old World. Ha ha ha!

Now I am a war criminal. I suppose the Americans are the best custody to be in then; they tend not to prosecute those . . .

She turns over in her sleep, then opens one eye. The eye is still asleep, but perceiving. One of her spy tricks. I watch her eye and then she closes it again.

Rachel means ewe. Sheep girl. With her teeth white as the mountain. Following her nation into its new despairs. I with her.

A soldier opens the door.

"Come on," he says. "They want you." Rachel sits up. But he only takes me.

"Is America at war?" I ask him.

"With who?"

"I mean, did America declare war?"

"Wait here." He pushes me into another cell, fluorescent lit.

He closes the door, and a minute later David opens it. Beloved David.

"How are you?"

"I thought you were on the submarine."

"I was."

"Did they catch you?"

"No. I'm here voluntarily. It won't be as easy to get you out this time, I'm afraid. The Americans are upset. We haven't been sharing our intelligence . . . How is Rachel?"

"She's fine."

"The Americans have cancelled your passport. The Israeli government is considering doing the same. Especially since your mother is not Jewish. But that's not your main problem right now. I need you to remember: the boy. Where did you last see him?"

"Atop the minaret."

"Which?"

"In Jerusalem."
"What?"
"He was the muezzin."
"When was this?"
"In my dream."

55.

He stands at the ledge, looking down at the people in Jerusalem. His voice serves as a translation mechanism, between the divine and humanity. So do all voices, but the muezzin needs a good one. The practice begins, though it likely originates even further back, with Zoroastrian sun worship, whose priests performed several daily ringing of the bells.

Sound provides the hearer with one of the brain's most carefully guarded senses, so we can hear danger in our sleep. The translation of sound into meaning, so closely linked to survival, provides us with the juice of the earth, its intimate immediacy.

Don Juan, sing for me. I can see Byron in your eyes, under the hooded glow of the castle and the sea:

56.

"Where did you see him last?"

"I don't remember."

"We need to know."

"Who is 'we'?"

"We'll find him eventually. I thought, if you could go to him, and invite him to come visit us, he'd be safer."

"Where do you think he is?"

"In Gaza still. But we can't locate him."

"All right."

57.

Paranoia means, literally, "beyond the mind." The mind is, after all, built for certain conditions. And when those conditions are exceeded, the mind must move beyond them. Perhaps all growth accompanies madness.

Los Angeles is the most paranoid city in the world. Paranoids often speak of a secret map of the world, a pharmakon similar to the dream riddle whose answer must by necessity be lost on waking. One road on that map leads to Gaza.

I step over the rubble. Within minutes I am in the throng of people, heading to market.

This is something Los Angeles does not have, these throngs. But the feeling is similar. The coordinated hunt for secrets.

I show people the photograph of Don Juan. No one recognizes him. I can feel the invisible walls taking shape around me.

I must get them out. Don Juan, and my wife.

Judaism has been referred to as a "Great House." This is the literal meaning of "pharaoh": Great House. Though archaeology confirms the Jews were never slaves in Egypt, they borrowed from Pharaoh. Both houses since 1979 have agreed that Gaza should be strangled to death. But the victim will not die. Electrocuted and burnt and mangled, thrown under trucks and poisoned, beneath shattered buildings, the muezzin is singing:

I am singing too, in the street. Poets are conspirators in the Middle East. All emperors know their wisdom and their threat. I am singing Rumi.

- - -

I am staying in a cheap and noisy hotel. There is no internet, but there is an English newspaper, the *Daily Gaza*. An article describes a local religious festival honoring a patron saint of a local stream. The water is now underground, I read, but the festival follows its course above ground, starting this afternoon.

The coffee is extremely good here; I drink three cups of it, thanking the proprietor, who smiles.

In the street the festival has already begun, like a Catholic procession sans icon, singing as they wave their arms in their robes, headed slowly west towards the sea. The children are dressed as sea creatures, in bright blue and green colors. An event honoring Poseidon, I see. From their past in Crete . . .

I follow at a respectful distance, listening to the clapping and shouts from the children, who are fully in character, gazing out at their audience as though through five murky fathoms, considering prey.

I see Don Juan, atop the shoulders of a man, dressed in white, moving in the center of the procession.

They are accelerating now, as the water moves downhill so do their bodies. Locals have heaved some of the worst offending concrete boulders from the latest bombing out of the way to make room for the celebrants.

The Mediterranean Sea is young by geologic standards: only five million years. This places it at the dawn of the human race as well; some of our smaller forebears who were first trying their hand at walking on the ground (and avoiding eagles). You could say it was born with us. Twins.

The children divest themselves of their colors as they approach the water's edge and stream into the waves, laughing, and the women are ululating into the surf.

Mohammed means "the praiseworthy." Now they praise the sea.

"American man, we are meeting again. Ha ha ha!" But his eyes are so old now.

I embrace him. He smells of winter.

"They're looking for you," I say.

"But they will not find me!"

His friend regards me nearby, watching.

"Do you want to come with me? They sent me to find you."

"You're working for the Jews?"

"No. Yes. Not quite. For you. And for my wife. But if you don't come I'm afraid what will happen to you. I protected you last time, didn't I?"

"Come swimming with me. Then I will decide."

The water is as warm as blood.

58.

"Tell me. Did you know I would love you?" I ask her.

"Men usually do."

"But did you know that I would?"

"Yes."

"How?"

The barrier seeps below, below my eyes. The raft I am following of hers, into the river. It is black dawn and I am pushing the sesta. But we are still in prison.

- - -

Time is different here. Time does not exist.

Part 3
Prison

59.

David has betrayed us. But isn't it in the nature of Davids to betray? Isn't it what they were made to do, with their belovedness?

Perhaps all love is a betrayal.

There is no natural light here. Only fluorescents.

I was processed with the other thieves of the week, made to sit as on a long bench that curved back and forth, in a small room, wedged tightly against the man in front, and the man behind me the same. All these rituals of bodies, to move them into the light, and out (and out completely).

I did not get a trial. What would I have been charged with, in Israel? The arrest is enough.

- - -

I considered telling the guards that I have converted to Islam, so as to be allowed to listen to the recording of the muezzin. But I do not like all that bowing. I must be content with the music I can make with my own lips.

Rachel is being held nearby, I have heard. Perhaps she is being tortured. I like to think she is not, that I would feel it if she were. But I do not know.

I ask for lawyers, for the ambassador, but then I remember that I am stateless now. No one can help me. Except myself.

Me and the others.

--

Prison is related to the word "prize," in the sense of "taken."

Prisoners are the prize.

We have been taken. We are yours.

60.

"I want pen and paper," I tell the guard.

"What for?"

"To write a letter."

Time is slow; freedom is fast.

I write a letter to my wife.

9th March

Dearest Rachel,

It's strange, I feel I do not yet know you. What our bodies have known is still to be translated to our brains, perhaps. At least it is so with me. I hope this letter can be delivered to you. But still, it feels good to write it in any case.

I love you. There is that, whatever else. A thing which may be useless, but not to me. Otherwise I would not be here.

Tell me: why did you marry me? Was it some strange marriage of convenience? I won't be offended if it was. Well, it doesn't matter now.

Tell me how you are, and if you need anything. I'm sure you have better connections than me but I will try with the guards to get whatever you may need.

I think of you always.

I am yours—

Two days later I received a reply. I had never seen her handwriting before; it was strangely childlike, with large loops in the letters.

11th March

My love,

Why must you write to me? It is not enough that I must sit in this darkness without a man, but that you must write to me in it? Well, it is only more torture. Perhaps that is what you meant, yes? Then good. I accept it from you.

I married you because you are handsome. There is no other reason. None that I will tell you. I am proud to be your wife. Israelis do not believe in convenience. Convenient things are dead things. Why don't you know this? Well, you are new here. It is true that I needed your innocence. And you are still innocent. Thank you.

I must go now, I am tired.

Love,
Your Rachel

- - -

I am middle-aged. It is strange to me. Like childhood, it brings a narrowing of awareness. I do not seem to be able to remember anything; it is all receded. Only Rachel, and the war. Nothing else matters.

I have requested legal representation and my jailers say that an Israeli advocate will be provided, but no one has come.

Convenient things are dead things, she says. Perhaps that was why I came to Israel. I had tired of convenience.

When I get out of here, I am going to raise hell.

- - -

12th March
Rachel,
The guards must be romantics to deliver these letters to us. But I am

grateful to them. What have you been thinking about? I hope you are well.

How long do you think we will be held here? The guards will tell me nothing.

I forgive David for what he did; I know he must have been forced to do it. I would forgive you, too; if the opportunity arises, make peace with our captors. Tell them you have forsaken me, and will cooperate. I will be happy knowing that you are outside.

I seem to sleep all day now; the darkness helps me.

Don't be too long in deciding; it may be our time will run out.

Love,

Robert

- - -

It was a month before she wrote again. A month where I contemplated how hard one would have to bash one's head against the stones to break one's own skull.

14th April

Robert,

I am sorry to be so long in writing. Things have changed; they let me out for a time to assist them in a job. Now they've returned me. It was good to be out, though the work was not pleasant.

I've asked to see you; they may let me. Please, do nothing to upset them. I need to see you.

Hopefully soon.

Love,

Rachel

- - -

Languor rushes my heart and my soul. The paradise extends itself over me, with her. In her. But I fear drinking this sweetness will hasten other outside consequences . . .

"What have you done?" she asked me.

"What do you mean?"

"What is this?"

"This is us."

61.

It's nothing. I can say it's nothing. I can say she's nothing. Nothing, next to me. Little singularity sucking me in:

I could say I did it willingly, that it was intended, profane, and reasonable, a sure answer to an understood question, part of the logic of the life that had preceded my time with her . . . but I don't wish for such things.

If we could assign meaning so wantonly to all things, there should be no mystery left in the world.

She does not make sense, nor do I. Save in love.

What part of love makes sense? How is it different from war?

She is with me for two days; it's hard to tell the hours. They don't take me outside very often. My vision has been getting worse in this dimness.

I have asked for a lamp. At last they bring me a small reading lamp, with a rechargeable battery.

I write her poem after poem. But I will not show them to her, or to you. They are very bad.

I'm told I am to be transferred.

Where do you put stateless people? With the Palestinians, of course.
Where we can live and die together.

- - -

I am in a narrow cage. Made of
green metal. I have been drugged. I
can barely move; I am standing.
Through the grating, I see a guard's
face. I mumble something.

The guard is startled. He says in
Hebrew, to someone I can't see: "He's
awake!"

The guard looks in at me. Fear is
very bad in guards. I try to reassure
him, but my voice isn't working.

"Hruybbdy," my mouth says,
and now the guard is shouting.

They open the grating and then I
feel a needle in my arm.

- - -

I'm in the ocean, splashing. It's
cold. Rachel is somewhere nearby.
No, it's Sasha. Where is she? I can
hear her.

The sky is turning black.

- - -

I am awake. Strapped to a table. Fluorescent lights peer down at me.

They put something down my throat. I'm choking!

"Relax, relax," says a woman's voice. "There."

She removes her hand from my throat.

"We've got to get you ventilated. We thought we'd lost you."

Her face is frightening; the eyes, like the guard's eyes, are hiding something, something I can't see . . .

"Relax. You've been intubated. You can breathe easy now. You were suffering from an overdose. Those damned lugs put too much in your shot! Relax now. I'll be back."

Rachel, where are you?

I should destroy Israel. Bomb it off the map. Lay waste to the soil. Salt the earth . . .

How many kings have thought the same.

I try to sleep, but I can't with this thing in my throat.

62.

The days come in, the days come out, the days play pinochle on your snout. A big green day with rolling eyes comes in my stomach and out my eyes. My day turns a slimy green, and pus pours out like whipping cream. I spread it on a slice of bread .
. .

I spread it on a slice of bread . . .

Heal me, Proust, give me your orange cookie, so I may escape. Let the cookie in, so I may be transported, away:

- - -

One day, and two. One day, and five, seven, nine, eleven, one day, and I am dying, somewhere where I remember why I came; one day and thirteen, though there are faces, the eyes follow me even when I am asleep . . .

No one asks me any questions. So I will tell no lies, great train, great train of Israel, churning mighty as the 20th Century, hideous deformed and screaming, iron horse withered and wrestling with the dawn, an angel with burning red eyes . . .

"Come on, open up."

They are feeding me.

- - -

Black isn't a color, it's a way of life, come in and see, these moments steep the rain of the mind, they soak the drift of the day, bodies are just numbers in a fragrant sea, of vampires . . .

I can see her face, but she's a demon.

"Rachel."

She's looking at me. She flaps her wings.

63.

I realize what they've done. They've told Rachel I'm ill, in need of special care. They don't want us to speak. I wonder if she believes them.

The room is yellow and white. Dull silver equipment and lamps.

The chair is beige polyethylene. Squeaking under my desultory shifting under my restraints.

"Awake, old man? Time for your next dose already?"

"No, no . . ."

"No?"

"No . . ."

The doctor is young, with healthy brown skin. His eyes shift back and forth, looking at my readouts.

"You're getting better," he says.

"Better . . ."

- - -

They take me outside.

They give me a cigarette.

I don't care what anyone says, tobacco is an aspect of god.

The light is like an alien being, washing over my face.

"Pretty day, eh?"

The nurse holds my hand.

There is a tree here. A date palm. The first tree humans domesticated, supposedly. It shines in the light and its fragrance filters into my nostrils. The cigarette tastes wonderful.

"Am I dead?" I say.

"No, still alive."

"Where is Rachel?"

"Is she your friend?"

"My wife."

"Oh, I didn't know you were married!"

"Yes . . ."

"We haven't seen her. Does she know where you are?"

"I don't know. Where am I?"

"Ha ha. We'll get you a phone. Hold on."

She puts a phone in my hand and then it rings. I answer it.

"Robert." The voice is official, and American.

"Yes."

"Back among the living, eh?"

"Who is this?"

"I'm Stewart Macintyre. I work with the White House."

"Oh."

"Your case has gotten some publicity lately."

"Oh."

"How are you feeling?"

"Excuse me a moment."

I lean over the edge of the wheelchair and throw up.

64.

"Where is Rachel?"

"She's your wife?"

"Yes. My wife."

"We'll see if we can find out for you. Relations between the US and Israel are rather tense at this time. But we want to see you released. The president may not be able to close Guantanamo, but we'd like to be able to show leniency in a few international cases. Perhaps including yours."

The day is still bright overhead. I raise my hand to the nurse. She hands me another cigarette.

"Go fuck yourself," I tell him, and hang up.

I draw the smoke into my lungs, and close my eyes.

- - -

The days roll in, the days roll out, but they've taken me off the drug. I don't know why. They give me all the cigarettes I can smoke. I smoke too many. Sometimes I can hear Rachel's voice in my head, far away. I close my eyes and listen for it, but whenever I listen for it, it recedes.

Is it any wonder I am this man now? To be dissatisfied with everything. No, it isn't that. It's love; this horror.

65.

They bring me a lawyer, an Israeli one. He contends I should plead guilty, and sign a paper. The paper is in Hebrew. I ask for one in English. He goes away. I do not see him again.

They bring me another lawyer, weeks later. This one speaks better English; he sounds Australian.

"What am I being charged with?"

"You have already been convicted, in absentia."

"Of what?"

"Terrorism."

"What is this place?"

"A medical center. Compassionate care was granted on the grounds of insanity. Because you're an American."

"How do I get out?"

"That's complicated. This is my number. Now that I've seen you, I can confirm to my NGO that you are alive and being held on charges. We'll see what we can do."

"But I am a terrorist."

"I'm looking for your wife too. But there is no record that she ever existed. Mossad isn't fond of sharing information, as you can imagine."

"Don't bother looking for her. If she wants me, she'll find me."

66.
I jump the fence.

67.

But certain prisons follow you no matter where the walls are.

I hitch a ride to Gaza. You don't need documents to get in; only to get out.

\- - -

I find Don Juan's family in the ruins. Cooking dinner over their fire. I hold the boy against me. His father offers me some of their food. I'm too ashamed not to take it.

"What are you doing here, huh?"

They smile at me.

\- - -

Gaza means "force" or "strength." I who desire the overthrow of so many governments now, lament that we can only barely govern ourselves.

"What now, senor?" I ask Don Juan.

"America."

68.

Jumping fences to America is harder. Don Juan takes me to meet his boss.

We duck under the tunnels lit partially by candlelight, and then he knocks on a dwarf of a door. A window slides open and he speaks in Arabic. The door opens and Don Juan bows, gesturing me inside. I take off my shoes and sit on the rug.

"Tea?" the man says.

"Thank you."

"We'd like you to spy on America."

"Where do I start?"

69.

America rides alone, on her long fury, work ruler, ruler of work, tyrant and king, megalomaniac surprise, ancient evil, champion of strange events, Amerigo, Amerigo, Amerigo…

Nations are strange things. I understand Benedict Arnold so much better now. You can be more loyal to an idea than to a people. What an American idea!

I am shaving my beard. For the first time in ten years.

How to help Palestine?

What weapons do they need? Not bullets and guns, I believe. But something more radical. The right idea.

Amerigo, yield to me, you tyrant, lend me space on your great boat, and I shall row too, into the horizon:

**Part 4
America**

70.

I have an office. The walls are brick; it used to be a manufacturer of children's games in the 1920s. I look out on the city below, in the snow.

I have never been more alone in my life. Or more afraid. The feeling is thrilling too, like a boy's adventure, and the thing about boy's adventures (maybe girls too, I can't say), is that they stretch to an almost infinite point, but not quite infinite, just limited enough that you can sense your own hand in their resolution, the world small and large enough to accommodate your imagination, and your trials.

I am a contractor for a religious association, distributing pamphlets to churches around the country. Mostly the secretary does that, a battle-axe of a woman with steely eyes and voice who drinks herbal tea and swears. Her name is Cynthia.

Cynthia and I have the office suite to ourselves. Us and the snow.

My name is Timothy Wiltback. I am thirty-seven years old. My wife is deceased. I am a bachelor. I live in a small apartment on Third Street. I wear a tie to work. I drive a 2004 Toyota. I pay in cash.

Something is coming clearer to me: what it is I must do. To spy is to see; the best stories are the ones that see the most, and make its truth from those things seen.

I cannot bomb America to death, or assassinate its leaders. I can't poison all its water or lay waste to its land and crops. No man alive can rape enough of its women, kill enough of its men to end America. I can only change its story. That is my job: storyteller. Propagandist.

The best story wins.

71.

Step one: establish a Jewish homeland in America. There is more land here; not enough in Israel. We are their closest friend anyway; why not give them some land?

And since possession is nine-tenths of the law, the first thing is to convince enough Jews to secede.

The Palestinian Authority has purchased some land in Iowa, with me acting as agent. Iowa's land area is seven times greater than Israel's. I'm sure the Hawkeye State can be convinced to part with some of its rich loam for the sake of the Jews.

"Where do we plant the sweat lodge, Tim?"

"Anywhere you like."

Me and ten hippy Jews. It's enough for a minyan.

Alder trees, young and flexible, bent into a dome. Rocks heated all day, on ground clear of duff, so that the fire will not spread into the soil below. Not smooth river rocks, as those will explode in the heat. Rough rocks.

For the Sami in the frozen north the sauna had its own spirits, and there is a natural logic to the chants we do in the steam; singing to the cosmos.

Rachel is in my body somewhere, like a friendly tumor, or pregnancy. As I sing.

\- - -

I have bought a full page ad in the New York Times. The headline: *A New Jewish Homeland!*

We are buying more of the adjacent farms. Kosher meat is good eating.

The kibbutz is not a primitive one; we have showers, and hydroponic marijuana, and an indoor recreation room with a ping pong table. The money flows from Washington, to Jerusalem, to Gaza, and back here to Iowa.

Follow the money, and be healed. Ha ha ha!

Cynthia has created a new brochure, along with the innocuous Christian pamphlets that provided me with my cover story. The New Jerusalem. In Iowa farm country.

I want to look for Rachel, but know I shouldn't. I may be a strange kind of spy, but I still can't go around advertising it.

Can I hire someone instead? No. I have to wait.

- - -

Summer has come to Iowa. Tell me I am worth this endeavor, and that this endeavor is worth me, if only to set my hand to the work more fully; if only so I can begin to heal after these horrors. Horrors which include me.

Tell me that these events are my offspring, only in part but a necessary part, ones necessary and true, inexplicable perhaps but still clear, seen and made ours. Tell me that I am here for a reason, a reason that is Rachel's, not only mine.

Tell me Israel may move, as she always has, for the Jews in their ancient wisdom do not ascribe to the obligations of Jewish husbands that they provide roofs for their wives, only sex and food and clothing, knowing that the sun and earth will turn over them soon enough, obliging a change of household . . .

My minyan understands. But we need more. America is full of failed experiments; half rotten with them; and this one must succeed.

Come to Iowa, O Jews, here in the heartland of America, so that my deeds might have meaning, and so that these failures could be merely the foam on your coming sea:

72.

The Canaanites are coming. Here in the new land of milk and honey. Promised land of the Unites States government. New Indians, over the plains:

Ten thousand kibbutzim by post email and Facebook message, by pigeon and by railcar, private jet and mule, by heel and umbrella, weathered and free:

Canaanites come here by fire rain and sleet summertime ends, raucous as all Jews are raucous, stewed and pickled and absurd, in our modern America:

"Quite a show you have here, Mr. Wiltback."

"Call me Robert."

Settlers again.

73.

Though it should have happened other times, perhaps, and not to me, it was anyway, and this has been my story. In becoming a spy I learned something of the power of words I had not known, when I was a boy, or even a man, and coming to them later in life is both a privilege and a handicap, for having learned all I had to then, and all I would learn later.

This document, such as it is, suffers too for this obstinacy in a late learning: that I could have done more, I know, and so I must exploit its limits so some of its absences can thrive and grow into something it would not otherwise be.

Even a horrid little tale such as this is, of monsters and their fields, is of a kind, and it must, if only out of habit, follow that course and make its music in turn, so that you will know when to sing along, and when to keep silent—suggestions, and patterns, for your feet, on the dance floor of literature.

It isn't enough, what I did, because I had done more evil than good, and what came after my strange resolve to help the people of Palestine by welcoming the Jews, once again, as we had perhaps not well enough before done, to America, America, America, so I must take this time in Iowa to write words inadequate but at least aspirational, to the task at hand.

Because Iowa is a special place.

And I am a special man. Otherwise I would not write this. Ordinary people do not write down the stories of their lives. Or not enough. Such is the lament of the historians, but it is so.

And so this wine is for Israel, a people of wine, and also for Iowa, that land that took in the Jews again.

Taking in the Jews again, for when it's time to welcome Jews, you know you must be doing something right.

74.

Jews, Jews in the field.

Jews, and Jews in the field.

The Jews are in the field, with their harvesters, and their goats.

I am here too.

Over the heavens are geese, and there is a blue sky.

Children have come, too.

Rachel is gone away but I am here, improbably. Here, improbably, at last, a man no longer of his country—his nation—but perhaps at last a man of country, who has dirt under his fingernails and knows something about trees.

Jews are men of mine and also trees, with those old cedars of the Lebanon, and we set as medieval French peasants making bocage onto the land, putting the pigs out of the terrible silos and letting them eat under the sun, for which they were grateful.

Like so many things it was simply done, and all the planning had not been enough, and it was good that there had not been too much, but simply announced.

Jews in the field of Iowa rhyme me too, for they see me for what I am, this broken man, now come home, to a home of my invention.

The children are the best because they know too, but they forgive me what I am, the haunt of the pasture, a kind of jack-o-lantern, known for his faults, but an important part of the landscape, and remarkable for that.

Remarkable to be alive despite the enormous efforts of governments and thousands of years of prejudice working as they do to kill men, women and children in their thousands.

And good on America too, simply the size of the continent. The thing Americans forget in our grand paradise, of so much land under our feet.

And so I have left America after all; the Orthodox are happy because there can never be enough Israels for them, for if the Messiah comes, who knows what terrors he may enact in the Holy Land to see what his servants have forgotten in his long absence, and some Jews of various stripes can then be hidden from his terrible Sauronic eye in Iowa corn fields, which must be the logic of all life, after all: why not try it over there?

Why not try it over there, where things are different, and a little of a different color, a radiant neighbor patch of sky, and plants not known before, this sea by your eye and match, as Cornwall or Dover or the eglantine of the heather under my ancestors' feet, must have come known to them at last as they arrived, from the Middle East also, wanderers.

Americans, being these terrible experimenters, do not object too strenuously to the loss of some of Iowa to what the racists call The Jew Reservation.

Jews are Being Reserved.
We hold The Jews in Reserve.
Here in Iowa Town.
In my heart.

75.

In each furrow is my heart, and each moment of the wrath of the elements can be visited in extraordinary ways to a farmer's eyes.

I smoke marijuana in the evenings from our hydroponic farm and the kibbutzim smile affectionately at me, their retarded Moses.

Moses was always retarded. This was why the Jews loved him.

And there is no better place for a retard than Iowa, a place far enough behind the times that the term can still be used with no particular resentment; some people are smarter than others, and this is okay. Fuckups in other states can be here merely stolid reminders of the cruelty of god, and his agents, men, and not thought ill of because of it.

And no one loves reminders better than Jews, who would remember everything.

Or, so I like to believe. Having undertaken to write this story makes me hanker for such a power of memory; one I do not, unfortunately, possess.

We are growing something in Iowa. For one, corn that isn't copyrighted by Monsanto. And eating that corn are these people I feel I've made, though really they've made me.

But outside, all my crimes are chasing me down . . .

76.

Let me remain in Iowa a time, and play with children. Let me drink wine and smoke marijuana. I shall be saved, by the elements, and by the people of this land, Jews and Gentiles, all the ancestors of my time here on this earth.

I will swim, and I will walk on this absurdly flat territory in the middle of the continent, completely solitary, like a hippy and hairy Wordsworth absent any romantic outcrops and sea spray, but just corn, and then corn, and then corn, over the corn, all maize of a thousand generations made up and made again, for the preservation of some innate delight, which is the sense of Midwesterners, that they have come here, and they shall not leave.

For indeed, I said we bought the farms, and so we did, but the truth is that many of the farmers were glad we did, as so many had not been owned by human beings for decades now, and to have human rather than paper owners was, at least, human.

Palestine made Israel once; for those Canaanites had fallen in love so hard and terribly, so profoundly and remorselessly that they invented a religion to hold on to it.

And having made Jews once, Palestine can do so again, making Jews again, for they are needed; I need them.

I need more Jews and we are making them here in Iowa, under bells Christian and Muslim, Zoroastrian and pagan. Some of them are brass and some are gold.

I drive the 2004 Toyota.

I smoke cigarettes again.

I am getting old.

But I am still alive.

And somewhere, out of the Israel of Iowa is my wife, with her knife.

77.

The Fifth Intifada was the worst, but that it should come and succeed was at least a worthwhile endeavor; and still we are learning what it is coming to be.

78.

What is vengeance, if not a kind of love affair? And what am I, if not a weapon in a war I will never understand? Vengeance of the elements against dark matter, and the universe against its own cousin, or its descendants, fighting for space, memory and time, and yet; oh, and yet;

Perhaps I have it wrong. That it is not vengeance at all; only love. And that vengeance does not exist at all, and is forgotten. Or, at least, modulated ever more tightly, so that its accomplishments are never so great as they might appear.

I know how badly the Jews want the promised land, because I want it, too. I want it to be here.

\- - -

In Iowa.

In Iowa.

In Iowa, O Ioway. I away I gone away, woman, don't come near. I gone some place no one can tell, and I ain't sure I comin back.

I know something though. I know these words, and the words of my new neighbors, all these insane neighbors, push against these envelopes of vengeance . . .

I have to keep running. If I run fast enough, I may not have to go back.

79.

Jews are dying in the Middle East, despite everything. Of course, some see justice in it. But it's a problem for me, as an absurdist adjunct of the new US government representative in the Jewish Commune of Eastern Iowa; I have to pick new and ever more complicated sides.

World peace is great, but too often it's a question of, in these shrinking numbers of deaths, still: who's it gonna be. The eternal and rich Jewish Police question: if we must cooperate in the dying, why not do it with eyes open?

- - -

I'm in my study, a small room in a log cabin we've built. A window looks out on the gardens.

A knock comes. "Come in."

It's Bashir, Don Juan's father. We embrace. I pour us both whiskey. I clink his glass. His dark face is grim.

"The Palestinian Authority has sent me. No one else could get a visa. The money has run out. We're proud to have helped our Jewish cousins and hope they'll do okay here now."

"What other news?"

"Don Juan—it's strange, I've adopted your name for my son—has vanished. I worry about him. But I know he's doing what he thinks best for Palestine."

"Are you all right?"

"I want to stay here. Apply for asylum."

"You're welcome to stay. It's probably best I don't sign any documents, but others here will."

"Thank you."

"Have you heard from Rachel?"

"No, I'm sorry."

- - -

The birds scream mad outside; fall seeds arrives and they swirl in great batches around the kibbutz. To take my mind off everything, I start another article for our newspaper, *Kibbutzim*: "Kosher Combines."

80.

I am driving the tractor with Mathilda. Her braids remind me of the spiral arms of the galaxy. The tractor is so loud we can't hear each other, or our thoughts. We are just highly vibrated squirrels atop the machine, cutting into the earth.

Vrum, vrum and vrum, my son, so you can be born too, though I am unworthy of it, and could have done better, it is appropriate that my situation is ridiculous, so that you will be, comparatively, masterful. Wise. Strong.

That you should be born is my right, says the man, and I shouldn't deny it. I should not inflict such sadness against my birthright, which is only to be a man.

Mathilda means "strength in battle," a good Jewish name. All these warriors. In our blood.

- - -

"Yes, yes, yes!" she's shouting.

- - -

She is like a small apple, brown.

Round and well-heeled. Polished and fragrant. She tastes like peat.

- - -

Cedars of the sinning Sinai beneath thy moon and underneath all moons, swirling round us, each light year cometh for our strength, lit up over thy skin, to lightning:

She touches my hair.

81.

I want to go and hunt for my wife, and for Don Juan, but I can't bring myself to, not yet. There's too much to do here, and also, I am afraid.

Perhaps this story is for my son.

Son, your father was a royal fuckup, a malcontent no-account fraud, a murderer and war criminal, who killed one nation and made another. Son, I'll do anything for you; I'll kill more countries, if that's what's needed, and that's part of the problem, this terrible urge, urgently pushing the mind to yet greater feats of blood and vengeance…

Son, the world is wrong and while I am too, I've been working to change it all, me included, for your sake, so you don't have to put up with all this horrendous bullshit.

Son, the Jews are assholes, but they're our assholes, and they're the only people I know who worship words, so whatever else they've done wrong, the future cut into rock, wood and stone resembles their own tribe and my work must at least include the necessary acknowledgment of that.

You can never have enough Israels. Especially of the mind.

Son, be better than me.

82.

In the sweat lodge, rocks and water. We can remember the directions, and the circles, what the Indians whom we decided, praise God, not to kill off, knew better than us, and the Romans too—this magic of the world not lost in the Age of Reason but transformed into something even more beautiful . . .

It is my privilege to be here. I want to be able to explain the enormity of it; of what it means. Like lightning.

We do not know what lightning is! Although we know it likely was instrumental in the creation of life.

I am chanting in the steam to honor the four directions. The dancing green woman...

Dancing Green Woman!

83.

I'm driving west, to see Jake. Not something I should do, but I also don't feel there's anything else to be done.

Mathilda is pregnant and my wife is nowhere to be found; one Israel gone and another founded; and I am a refugee within my own country, without papers or my name but still, in this fashion, inescapably American.

West to the sea and to my friend.

- - -

Passing the Largest Ball of Twine in the World, and the Dinosaurs Meet Jesus, and other Midwestern Paraphernalia Americana, to the mountains:

Pike's Peak and the Continental Divide, a divide of more than continents, and more than water systems, a division in the warp and woof of reality.

West:

Gas stations and McDonalds, despite Civil War and environmental disaster, rainforest collapse and moon landings, they are both survivors, like ticks, clinging to my socks . . .

And California, the Successor State, named for Muhammed, and for the future:

84.

"What do you want?" he says, standing at his door.

"To talk to you."

"Why?"

"Please."

We go inside. His same house, but it feels like a different one now.

"How are you?" I ask.

"I'm fine. What do you want?"

"I kind of want to get drunk."

"Ha ha ha!"

- - -

His face is familiar to me but his movements aren't; we're all different now, I know. If anything he can drink more now than before, and I less. I watch him put them back as my vision goes askew . . .

"I need your help to find my wife."

85.

The American road courses through me like heroin. We take turns at the wheel headed to all her old haunts in Los Angeles, though there is no reason why she would return here. Except that Israelis love Los Angeles.

The city punishes me, and her shelter is eternal. Even if extinguished in a nuclear blast, Los Angeles is like Jerusalem now, indestructible, no matter its physical form.

We knock on all the doors we know. No one has seen her. We eat tacos on Crenshaw under the blinding sun, rubber dust exhaust and smog filtered with a distant sea air, a cocktail finer than the finest mixologist's, a primordial soup ordinating the conscious mind as a gnomon does the sundial:

- - -

We stop at a convenience store for sodas and she's on the TV, smiling into the camera.

And an audience applauding.

"Can you turn on the volume?' I ask the clerk.

"It doesn't work."

"Jake, look."

"She's in New York."

86.

I drift from sleep to waking and back ensconced inside the red eye, head bent as a penitent before our god, the East Coast, and its Oligarchs Regnant . . .

87.

New York is too much for me; I need to stand still. And these days, that is almost possible in New York; it has slowed down considerably.

"Come on, Rob. We're almost there."

Jake summons a cab with his phone and we are zapped west, through the nuclear fallout of Queens and Brooklyn, the freeway cut deep into the concrete and lumber houses, yawning before us:

"Why would she be on television, Jake?"

"We'll find out."

"It's something terrible."

"Maybe not."

- - -

I drink coffee under West Fourth. Even the "smoke smoke" man is gone; all the New York I knew as a young man. The city is now a kind of model home rental park, as one might see in the suburbs of Houston, with every corner freshly painted in the hopes of new renters, and fake televisions in the windows.

"The studio is at Lincoln Center, come on," Jake says, checking his phone.

At least the subway still feels similar—the last oasis before the storm of the future wipes the city off the map.

\- - -

She has an office. In Tribeca. The Lincoln Center people send us there. The office is on the seventeenth floor. I step out of the elevator with Jake and walk down the hall.

A secretary looks at me, goes back into her office. I walk faster, down the hall. I open her door. She raises her head and looks at me. Her hair in her eyes. She brushes it aside.

"What are you doing here?" I say.

"Producing."

"Producing what?"

"Sit down."

"You remember Jake."

"Hello, Jake. What I'm producing, Robert, is the war. Did you think that all we've done could so easily go away?"

The weight of the room settles in my shoulders, in the back of my neck. In my hands. I watch her face, her eyes.

"I have things to do. Meet me for lunch in an hour," she says, dismissing us and turning back to her computer screen.

- - -

Oligarchs regnant on my long summer, sweet, lovely, this New York message, that it is okay, we are here, eat at Joe's if you like, we don't care, we have Joe and we have you too, and this is our duty to both of you, you and Joe, that you should find each other, and we should be there to watch.

We eat at Joe's, across from her office tower, hamburgers and potato chips with some kind of herbal tea served in a strange pot.

"This is a good hamburger," I say, and she nods.

"It's good you two found each other," Jake says.

88.

Lightning inside. I am a puppet; I am this servant, not of her but of something I don't understand. Her apartment is like a bad 1980s movie, starring Johnny Depp, or Trent Reznor, with black and grey and silver and modern looking kitchen appliances smoothed by the hand of modernity, like an array of dildoes that can extrude coffee, eggs and toast.

I make them all and watch her sleep, I am a victor, and she is my servant, I can tell myself these things, and they are even true, though only the most superficial of observations.

I am a man and she is a woman, but I don't know what that means.

I crunch the toast in my mouth and she opens her eyes.

"Are we still married?" I ask.

She nods.

89.

I'm running again. In New York. A city I have never seen before, the way it is now. A prison, of course, but they all are, and what kind is this one?

All this positive energy. I suppose California finally invaded New York and they don't know what to do with it. It confuses them. And, in turn, New York invaded California, and we don't know what to do either. We're sad.

Running in New York and I'm married. Married and a murderer.

I guess I'll fit right in in New York.

\- -

It would seem I can't escape, but, is that what I was trying to do?

90.

I look at the man's photograph.

The Prime Minister in Exile's assistant.

Ending governments takes time; the idea resists the turn in your hand. Bend it tighter, and hold on, until your route kicks in.

It's okay to kill. This was the mistake of World War One; that they had not remembered. It is okay.

The gun is in my pocket.

Overhead, the sun.

The city remembers me from my youth. But I don't remember it.

Planning to kill has a way of attenuating the mind; in part because the mind is a killing machine and so devotion to this act brings all its parts into full operation.

New York, triumphal killer, feels more at home to me now, in the eyes of the men and women, even some of the children, tightened down hatches and hunger boiling the blood, to the ferocious street-level pitch . . . lucky coin . . . lucky coin . . . no snake eyes . . . come on:

Red is the color of the season; the women look like tattered flaps of flesh, fresh from the butcher, long legs and dark hair, hats and sunglasses and shoes and purses, the bourgeoisie, the ongoing religion embedded in every step of the people, known before time began, in their light-footed stares and turns, ritual laughter and burns, heated to the exchange of gravity and feet, turning at corners and stairwells, binding the heat of the furnace to some god who has never been named . . .

There really are a lot of women wearing red today. I get up and walk, waiting for Rachel to summon me home, unwilling to end the man's life today.

91.

Long love in a towel, coffee and the occasional cigarette; she wants me and wants me to follow orders. In some ways, everything is highly appropriate. I've found my niche — expatriate killer — and the universe has responded with these pleasures and absences, this nice apartment, and the calm I haven't felt for years, not in Los Angeles, or Israel. The nihilism of New York suits my mind now, but I know it can't last . . .

"What happened to the old New York?" I ask the coffee man.

"You're looking at him! You want that white or black?"

- - -

Mathilda is due in three weeks; I book a flight.

92.

Lilt and lull, my son, and I am yours, whatever else may be I am still yours, absent nation or language, religion or history, I am yours, hindered and sent to for you, holding your mother's hand, in the hospital.

If I should be yours, let it be complete, and let my weapons be stronger than my enemies', and more concealed, and let them thunder under my wrath beneath the sky, unlimited, as a god's wrath, unstoppable, full of fluid and noise, bringing new life:

93.

I am a father. Mathilda is asleep with the boy on her chest.

94.

Though it should be love, it's something else, or, if you like, one form of it we do not have the words for; but it's my job, find words, old son, make it happen:

I am alone.

I make love to Mathilda and fly back to New York. I retrieve my gun from the locker at the station and go hunting.

95.

He is forty-eight and lives now with his mother on East 72nd Street.

"Winter's coming quick," I tell the doorman.

"Yeah she'll be here before too long! Me, I got retirement in six months! Florida's waiting for me. Hahaha."

"Good for you."

"Can I help you with something?"

"Yeah, where can I get a good sandwich around here?"

"Right across the street. I love those pastramis in there. Can't eat em anymore, though. Aggravates the colon!"

I sit across the street and watch the Manhattanites parade while I feast on my thirteen dollar sandwich.

- - -

He comes out at night, holding an umbrella, the old fashioned kind with a leather handle shaped into a curve.

Governments are directions. Why can we not be cows, who govern by simple democratic vote? Each standing in turn to point her nose towards the chosen horizon. No demagogues ever contravened the cows. But we seem to await demagogues, hoping a new loud-mouthed ape shall arise and lead us, relieving us of the burden of thought, in a great parade, our bodies linked in a timeless fabric of violence.

I put a round into the chamber and follow him, but I will not kill today. He stops at each corner and looks around, like he is trying to remember something.

I make eye contact with him once, but his gaze slides over me. He's looking for something. I follow him north to 80th Street. He makes a right and then slips into a Chinese restaurant.

I light a cigarette across the street and watch him sit down at a table with a man.

Night comes over New York and over my soul too.

96.

Rachel is distant, but still warm, her eyes intent on some new purpose, which she will not share. Her broadcasts are going well, I think.

I stroke her hair in bed and ask: "Honey, what's your show about?"

"Why don't you watch it?"

"I can't stand to watch the TV."

- - -

New York, by my mother, nearest to God, a dying one, nearer every day. I miss my Los Angeles.

Planes, buildings and torrents of *frisson*, so French you could shit, but it has no *je ne sais quoi*, because they know everything now in New York, and in knowing everything they've killed epistemology dead, it is no longer possible to know anything in New York; they've died, and my job is to hasten its destruction.

Just one more dead oligarch. Why should this one be harder? Because I'm a father? Because what we've done is starting to get much bigger than a little revolution is a small Middle Eastern country? Because the love in my heart is corrupting my body, and making me do things that don't serve my politics, or even my own life?

I listen to Rachel's LPs with my headphones on, Radiohead and the Red Hot Chili Peppers and Norwegian screeching bands and Glenn Gould and I run, I run around the block, waiting for the ticking time bomb to come down to zero, come down to zero, my little time bomb of my heart, make me do this thing.

97.

Tell yourself it's what you need. And you do need it. Tell yourself it's natural. And it is. It will become natural as soon as you do it. Everything that exists is part of Nature.

Tell yourself you want it. That it's part of you, the you you're becoming.

And tell yourself it's all right. And it will be. As soon as you get it done.

Get it done, and by fire and ice, we shall be healed, in the long goodbyes from American memory. This too is American—jettison memory—and come with us into another world. A world of grievance, fire, and revolution.

Come with me, though your heart may say you should not, quavering: come with me, and though it be all right, I will be there for you, to whisper a word in your ear, of when to fire. And you can. You can fire. Because it is justice.

Justice is fairness but fairness is beauty. And so both justice and beauty are this kind of average. Just like the tax board in California, hmm. Just a little board of equalization.

Beauty and truth.

Why do you think Don Juan died in that Greek revolution, hmm? One can't write poetry and not want to kill.

98.

He's on the floor, blood pouring out of his shoulder.

I'm calling her on my phone.

The New York I knew is gone.

Part 5
Israel

99.

Like beauty and justice, the Middle East knows about the Middle. Oh, poor overlooked Middle Child. Our dear Lisa Simpson, with your saxophone and suicide bombs. (Iowa is the perfect place for the new Jewish State, being in the Middle.)

Old Israel falters but does not fade. It is too well armed to fade.

I'm not sure killing the representative of the government-in-exile did anything, but Rachel assures me it was invaluable, that our goals are closer to being reached.

We are back in Jerusalem. It is enough like Los Angeles that I don't feel homesick.

- - -

People are the problem everywhere . . . under any government . . .

Too few want to govern, and those that do are mad . . .

Burnt light and summer dreams of the new Palestinian Parliament are overshadowed by summary killing in large numbers. Where the Jews could not abide a non-Jewish state, the Palestinians seem unwilling to abide the reverse. But like Israel at its founding, the new Palestine is ostensibly secular and ethnically inclusive . . .

I've told Rachel I've had enough killing and so now she is the one who has to do it. Jews killing Jews. My compromise is that now I am the propagandist, writing articles to be translated into Hebrew and Arabic describing the viciousness, paranoia and disorganization of the Zionist revolutionaries fighting the new state. Like all the best propaganda my words are entirely true; the art is in what you don't say.

\- - -

I go to Tel Aviv, unable to bear Jerusalem any longer. Lilt and fade, old son, for though the government may fall, the culture lives on, in the night club and steps of the people, nods and wiggles and long dark looks, under the rim of the ocean.

Take me, and let me escape. And though I will not be remembered, my deeds will, separate from me, as though they were acts of the universe itself.

I hold the hands of the dancers in the dark and close my eyes. The music is a kind of engine, and also a sculpture, making the right angles in the air, even as our oldest temples arranged space and stone in Gobekli Tepe so as to provide a particular sensation in the body . . .

The world continues to grow on the seeds of a broken heart, says the singer, tumbling over the waves of the strings.

100.

In another woman's bed. What have you done, Robert? Not with this woman, but in general.

The ocean and the highway and the pretty young woman's face. The sensation that I have been robbed. Perhaps I did it myself.

The weight of the region grows; I have only increased its burden. Atlas expands. The world with it.

I speak to my son on a video call; he is happy in Iowa.

I feel guilty for so many things; but the world seems to keep forgiving me. Why is that?

And what, exactly, is the punishment that I crave instead?

101.

When I will live. When I will die. When I will live again. I drive back to Jerusalem. The guards don't even blink now at my Israeli passport. The borders have become porous.

This woman. Sheep woman. Her teeth fleece, cheeks jewels, hair bordered in silver, her cluster of camphor. Thy dove's eyes.

Black dove.

Dear black dove, fly with me, and take me away from this world, and all of its works, so I might be free. So I might never need do anything again.

The beams of our house are cedar, and our rafters' fir. Our bed is green.

Black dove, be with me tonight, and tomorrow, fly.

102.

The dove Columbiforme. Named so for its diving. So too was Columbus a diver, off the deep end, into new worlds.

Dive with me, black dove, off of the edge of the bridge, and see the world.

103.

You are black, but comely as the tents of Kedar. Black as our curtains. The bundle of myrrh between your breasts. Between your legs.

Feed among lilies and let me die. I will feed them too.

104.

Black dove, come with me. No matter where, but away. Take off your gauntlets and let go your fine steed, and remove the jewels from your hair.

The house of cedar and fir is pulled down, and set fire. Your hair is shaven. The smoke and the dust have blown over us, staining our clothes and our skin.

But you are black as a dove and drive on through any storm, hearing my heart.

Come through this storm with me and I promise you, by my troth, and my balls, by my hair, and my eyes, that I will comfort thee on the other side, and on the mountain after that, when we will see the whole world we have made, never to pass again, but still here, for us, for some moments, to stain your face with the sun, and the light of your laugh shall rain on me for days and weeks after, years after, even when I am alone.

"Rachel?"

"What is it?"

"I'm coming home."

"Well, hurry up. I have things to do."

105.

Jerusalem is quiet. Parliament is in session. Falafel on the street. Prayers in the various houses of worship. All submissions steles carefully oriented, towards various sky and earthly fathers and mothers, all Great Houses owed their obeisances and duly paid, yet and still, just as the Palestinians have been paying Egypt for 6,000 and more years.

I get one of the falafels and watch the street. In their Achaemenid devotions. Parkour and tai chi. Embattled, but more gloriously alive than ever.

The etymology of Palestine is "rolling," referring to Crete's conquest of the Mediterranean's eastern shore. So too our older cousins colonized it first, deciding once there was enough oxygen to make a break for it, balls out, and inhale the open air, of Earth.

My black dove is flying over the city. In my mind's eye, I can see her, fluttering, swift as an arrow, diving:

I go the movies instead. I'm trying to learn Arabic.

106.
I am counting. But when I reach zero, what will happen?

107.

Achaemenid is the Latinized version of Persian *haxamenes*, "having a friend's mind." This is appropriate since we understand Assyria absorbed the previous empires surrounding them, adopting many practices and innovating others.

Women, we know, seem to have been the chief victims of modernity; with each passing millennium, the religions and laws have tended to include greater and greater restrictions on women. The veil, which in Babylon was worn by women only during the marriage ceremony itself, became an institution in Assyrian times (about 3500 years ago), to distinguish between noblewomen and slave women. Property owning women were legally bound to harems, in their wealthy gardens.

The instinct seems intimately tied to agriculture; subduing nature and subduing women have gone hand in hand for the last 10,000 years of our history.

108.

And even now, I know I can never leave. Israel has crawled inside of me.

109.

The weight of the earth, like the weight of marriage, depends upon a fusion of opposites. This day, my heart, and the next, my legs. The diminution of the body's capabilities, set off in some instances by a broadening of the mind (or a narrowing of it), only the big bang to usher in new forms of life.

But the problem with statistics is they deal with large numbers. It is certain that a particular number of people, depending on locale, die by gun violence in a given year. It is an unlikely circumstance. And in any array of danger, of course, statistically, you have a set of odds for survival.

But these statistics are the boiled down essence of the raw stuff of drama: before you are a statistic, the only person who determines your survival is you and your immediate neighbors (friendly and otherwise).

What is the worth of your survival? This survival (literally, *living over* . . .), this victory . . . win the world, but then make that world what you want, what you thought you needed, and that world, your creation, is your worst enemy.

I take the train to East Jerusalem. I visit Don Juan's bombed house. His family safe in Iowa now, with the New Israeli Jews. But where is Don Juan?

The corner store that sold beer is shut, too.

The city watches me from its infinite series of squares. Windows, plazas, street corners, the maze . . .

I light a cigarette and watch.

When I was a young man, I would watch the magic of the cigarette.

Baby, let me stand next to your fire . . .

"Are you American?" a woman asks me.

"Not anymore."

"Curse you," she says in Arabic.

"God bless you," I say.

Of course it is naïve of Americans to believe a change of government would change the people themselves.

Naïve, meaning, at root, native. Naïve Americans. Native Americans. Us and our nativism. If you ignore facts hard enough, can the ones you prefer become the truth?

I smoke the cigarette and watch the sun move down the sky. I've never felt more like a spook. Like I can sink into the stonework and sheer my face into the rictus of a gargoyle, which only means "gargle," gargling the rains of the storm until they bleed my face white and shapeless.

110.

"This boy," I say in English. "Have you seen this boy?" I am asking at the police station.

"Speak Arabic," says the policeman.

"This boy," I say again in English, "Have you seen him."

"No," he says, in Arabic.

"Do you know him?"

"Who are you?" he asks in English.

"A friend."

"Are you reporting him missing?"

"Yes. I want to report him missing."

"Fill these out," he says in Arabic.

The roving Jewish gangs have been getting worse. Some of them are paid by the government in exile but many are "home grown." Their methods have proved as diverse as the Palestinians before them, bombs, knives, pipes, cars, anything blunt, sharp, explosive, projectile, or otherwise dramatic . . .

Drama is the door out of statistics.

I fill out the papers and go back on the streets. I show people the face of Don Juan, in my photograph.

111.

Feed among the lilies.

"Was it you who came in last night?" Rachel asks me, in English.

Upon the mountains of Bether, you are a stone.

"Yes. You were expecting someone else?"

"I didn't know who it was."

"Yes, it was me. Do you not remember?"

"I have to go out tonight. Be my second."

- - -

No, in the valley of the lilies be not afraid, for the field itself will comfort you, in its rising mist, and the heat and hatred of a generation, be like a wind, over your forelocks, making divine music:

She is in the café. I am on the street. I've become more dangerous; I'm starting to look at least part Israeli.

Don't ravish my heart too bad; I am only an American. We abhor ravishment of all kinds; we seek quiet;

solitude. But here this city and its hundred ancient tongues thundering:

I can see the look in his eye all the way across the street. A basement dweller. A revolutionary.

He's raising his hand to her cheek.

112.

Be the roe of the field. For my black dove soars in the light, and wherever her light guides her I am there, no star nor fire. Neither here nor dead, but a shadow, like death but eternal. Because Death can't stop quitting on us.

Running in Jerusalem is like studying the Torah. How far back to you want to go?

Are you sure you want to run?

113.

Elijah, I await thy boot, on my neck. Here, I have fastened the chair to the ceiling. Sit there. And let me witness your death on the stones.

Black dove; black dove; run to the hinterland; I am waiting there; after Jerusalem falls.

114.

Running in Jerusalem is like studying the Kabbalah. Amongst its other qualities, the lesson of the Kabbalah is how to survive nightmare; how to identify its edges; how to reason with its ghosts.

This world, which we like to think so solid, is anything but. It is only a pool on a mountainside, ready to be hit by any asteroid you name. Or any frog, come to sleep by our side, and croak. Both are equally dangerous.

To run in Jerusalem is not like running in Los Angeles. They are many thousands of years apart. Running in Jerusalem runs down an ancient empire, a word which means "lay down," like strata, the geologic morphology of a nation, and a region.

Here in the endless night. Is it a door you wish to enter?

Go in; see what lies in side. Jerusalem is a religion of doors. Some you can't come back from. Each of them, you will be changed by.

Focus, and forget. And listen to the sounds of the night.

Women make the best spies because they love men. She kisses him but breaks it off and looks behind; she sees me. He does not. And they're running.

Black dove, I am behind thee. Invisible against the sun. Give me your war.

And then let me go. You are inside me. Hovering over the sky.

115.

I am a madman, but this is because I have been chosen as her tool. What anger may be in her service is useful. What regions I've known, because of her.

Even if it is not so, it is so. To decide opens so many doors that the gravity wells which are the doors of the Middle East cannot but keep you running; you are too well wanted.

It is not *Enceiderich, jetzt oder nicht,* but merely, decide.

You will get a second chance. And a third. And a fourth. You will have decided anyway.

I am banging on the door.

He is undressing her. I'm kicking the door.

I'm breaking it.

And now here inside she clasps his neck and I kick him in the balls.

Violence means "to pursue with rigor or desire."

Charting paths through the estuary of Jerusalem, who better to follow than a bird? Aegis of the night.

"What did you think, little scoundrel? That you'd be the chosen one?"

I kick him again.

"Stop Robert. Let him talk, he wants to tell us something."

But all that comes out of his mouth is vomit.

116.

Hunting revolutionary Jews. Hunting the celebrated. Servants of changing empire.

Change my empire with me, cousin, and I will lay down the sheets and light the perfume. I will sing songs of the sea. I will kiss your mouth.

Empire, prepared in order. From the Latin *parare*.

Make ready, prepare, furnish, provide, arrange, order, contrive, design, intend, resolve, procure, acquire, obtain, get, get with money, buy, purchase, set forward, meet with ease, don't frolic, be on your best behavior, set steady, set at warrant, make choices and be healed, on the right side of the pond, on the last estuary before the night, starboard and wash, port and sally, all rests on the last each reach before midnight, in the thousand names, and in the heat of the world, rest at midnight, count forward, and watch and wait, count ammunition, and philosophy, count slaves and women, count freedmen and mercenaries, count the sky, count the sky and set forward your watch, and mark your watchmen at time, mark your heat and your brow, and set forward the dove to fly, at my mark, fly at my mark:

He was the first, but there were others.

Set me forward, watchman, and I will be healed with each task. As I cleanse my body of your pollution like a good priest. Servant of empire, but which?

117.

Let me serve. The main route *Columbiforme*, cutting through the air. For life. Not in the sense of duration, but for purpose. Even if she leaves me, or I her, the purpose is everything.

Endure, and be healed, is the Jewish philosophy. Endure, longer than stone, and be healed. And if your holy mountain is torn down, another will arise, more holy, and you will have endured that too. Keep your head down. Do your work.

Set aside the bushel of wheat for the stranger. But keep your distance. Mind the boundary stones. And above, in the sky, Jews in Space are flying, Kabbalistic ghosts!

Jews in Space, like gods too, of all colors, as the rainbow, God's promise, fluttering in beauty through the continua of the universe, in reason and alone, far off, and over your head.

Servus, slave.

But the word may have been an Etruscan proper name, the people who enslaved the Romans, and whom the Romans later enslaved.

Urbs and *orbis*—city and circombinitant world—is too the revolution of empire and dissident, and this is service, to adopt the name of your master and then make the name a slave, in revolution.

Serve me in revolution, and hunt with me revolutionaries. And our wheel shall spin faster, faster and faster:

118.

Some have told me philosophy is a distraction. But wisdom only means to look, and see. What are you being distracted from?

119.

Still, the danger of philosophy becomes ever clearer to me. I understand now why religion too provokes violence; one needs it to assuage the mind against the horrors (and the beauty) of blood. Good warriors neither crave nor fear it, but exist on the boundary: appreciating its necessity and fearing its lure.

Like a woman.

Columbiforme, we have dived, and in the fall, we learn.

Black dove, arm me.

120.

The boundaries of the modern state do not exist on a map. They are not tied to geography. They exist in the mind. It is unfortunate that bullets cannot travel as fast as Facebook messages; it necessitates much travel for us.

I am Mossad; my cock nurtures the Garden of Eden that is the Earth.

I hold her hand on the coach flight over the Atlantic. The Federal government has encamped outside Davenport, demanding the surrender of one of the Jewish separatists.

It is Bashir.

121.
Bashir means "the one who brings good news." It is related to the Yiddish word "bashert," which means your promised and destined love.

We stars hear one another's voices across the gulf. We yearn, in our mystery, for the truth of our union. And we assemble many forces in our journey across time: so too you. Embedded in the web of the state of your body, turning to meet, love:

The officers meet us at the gate. No handcuffs this time.

"Getting rather familiar, aren't you?" I tell them.

Still, a nation sans borders is a tough customer to sell. It isn't enough to kill everyone who disagrees. Nor even to convince them. Like democracy, it appears to need conflict itself, for it is nourished by argument.

123.

Bashir's beard has grown. He stands in front of his field, shouting, at the federales and a couple of cameras:

"A lot of you are wondering what a Palestinian is doing here, defending our new Jerusalem! Here in the cornfields of Iowa! I tell you, I have as much right to be here as any man! And I have as much right to declare a sovereign territory as any of your founding fathers! I too am a founding father! And so is my wife Abra! And we tell you, government of Washington, that we love you! And we need you, far away!

"Your government and the government of Old Israel have collaborated for too long in the murder of my people. Now I too am a Jew; but this is not about religion. Our families are the same. What I have found in Iowa is peace, something I have longed for my whole life. And if you take it from us here, we will take yours from you too."

The megaphone shines in his hand. I hold my arm around Rachel's shoulders. Like parents at a softball game.

124.

We eat the comfort table of the Midwest, fatter than anything. Iowa means, "people of the south wind." Now we are in a lee, encouraging one another against the dying. Outside, pressure is dropping.

I raise my glass.

"To America."

What an absurdity.

"Is it true you are a hitman for the Israeli government?" asks an old farmer.

I smile and tell him, "I would never do something like that."

He laughs the big bellied laugh of one hundred and fifty years of corn.

Rachel's phone is ringing.

125.

Israel calling. Israel calling, over the wires. Israel, it's Israel again. Sarah, Sarah, won't you come over.

Sarah, Sarah, this laughter, what is it?

What is it Sarah, who is it, who is it heard you? Gentlemen? Gentlemen calling over the wires?

Servant of humanity and the earth, what stillness chills your brow? What migraine is coming?

126.

They are building a new Wailing Wall.

127.

Of course I have been a terrible father thus far. Is it possible to serve both a woman and country? Country is a cunt, as Shakespeare knew. So perhaps it's another way of asking: is it possible to serve both a very large and a smaller cunt at the same time?

128.

Fire; fire on the roses her thorns. Fire. Things have not been going well. But this is like saying: "we expected them to go well." No Jew thinks this way. No intelligent person either.

I am in a trench, with a rifle. In Jerusalem.

Check the breech.

Fill the magazine.

Push the bolt forward.

Close it.

The sight lines that had extended four thousand yards are now two hundred.

To believe in your cause is no small thing, but it does not do anything for you in war itself. It got you there; perhaps keeps you there. But it will not fight for you.

There is a sniper inside the destroyed building to our north. His name is Neshek, which means, simply, "gun."

But *neshek* can also mean "interest, or usury." Or, "bite."

"What is your interest here, peon!" I shout over the barricade.

He answers by firing.

"Do it again, he likes it," Don Juan says.

"Come get us, Mom cooked soup!" I shout.

For every Jew, twelve opinions. And the same with their armies. I believe Neshek is in a fundamentalist faction that believes the earth will end when the third temple is rebuilt; but I can't be sure.

"I'm going to run to that car. Fire when I do."

Light moves over the fluid of the city, exciting strangers to revolt. Cells automatic reflexive and autumnal exercise my boy in his cycling towards imminent disaster, of life.

Break and bear my new philosophy here to you, though I be killed; I am a messenger like all messengers of my own truth, whatever words my masters have delivered me here to say. I have seen gods on the way; I will tell you. They too are important, though we pass away from them.

Don Juan is screaming; he did not get Neshek. But, nor am I dead. I lob a grenade toward the window, but it falls short and I have to duck with my hands over my neck behind the car to shield myself from my own shrapnel.

I run again to the blown out door of the building and go inside.

I run up the stairs.

He's at the window.

He turns to look, and that look describes for me so much of this conflict; perhaps some aspect of conflict, violent or not, that I do not understand but am unable to escape. This embeddedness of it; that we are not what we think, and part of us knows this. Part of us will not reconcile the disparate haves, and the war outside begins with this war inside. Our mind elides the disparate forces which contain us but they are real, and sometimes one sees in someone's eyes that knowledge, that a new mind has taken over, quite without their consent.

Other men wiser than me have described the feeling of the gun itself; it is stronger than human beings, in its projectile power but even more in its psychological force. Like all tools it remakes humanity and we are actually in the service of guns, not the other way around.

This meme that will not die.

I shot him and watched some part of me leave too.

129.

Robby Junior is eating applesauce. He has it smeared over his face.

His mother is here, watching.

"Mmm, apple sauce," I tell the boy, and he smiles, and spits up some more of it.

I wipe it off his chin.

"I need some more money," she tells me, and I give her what I have.

130.

Of course, though we do not like to say so, part of America's love affair with Israel is because of religion. We are, despite everything, a Christian nation. Reluctantly so, but still. This terrible shell game. Shells make good knives, you know.

The word "re" is quite ancient, and it means "endowment" or "bequeathment." Reality is our endowment.

In religion, the "lig" is a tie, a bond. An enslavement.

So religion is our bequeathment of slavery. I don't say this in a negative way, despite appearances. Being tied up is a good thing. Being embedded. If you're part of life, you will have so many bonds. The question is: which ones do you want to keep?

131.

Of course bombs were the worst solution possible. If you can't be discriminating in death, how can you be in life?

Kill too many and you will be destroyed. Kill too few, and the same result.

Death is a machine, as so many have noted. Machines need tending. You mustn't make them go too fast. Or if you stop using them, they will break also.

Use it only so much.

Hold your foot gently to the gas, and accelerate to your chosen speed.

How fast do you want to go?

130.

I am a father, but what does it
mean?

131.

Those who become actors understand deception. All the world a stage. Those who become spies also. There is no master plan. There is only the moment.

My will, and my body, and the world.

Hunting is like religion, too. It is no accident. This tool of slaves to make reality bearable. To know what costs are likely, and how to adjust them.

We are celebrating corn. Organic corn, for the first time in a generation in Iowa.

My women are here. The mother of my son. And my wife.

Raise the stalks onto the barn for Sukkot.

Drink wine and let the world heal you. It is trying to.

132.

Don Juan has been injured. It is not a physical injury.

I visit him at hospital in Jerusalem, showing my fake ID to the guards.

Each flight across the Atlantic seems to make me sleepier. Now I am only barely awake.

I bring him chocolate and cigarettes and a newspaper.

"Captain," he says.

"You're the captain," I say.

"Captain, my wife, she needs me."

"Your wife?"

"My wife, she needs me. Have you seen her?"

"When did you marry?"

"She's here. I've seen her."

133.

Beatify my heat, kill fruitfully; let its fruits multiply your labor, kill well and swift and sleep a mighty warrior, on rest, on leave, when all the lights have nighted thee, in dreams. Rest easy and let no one want; let no one leave. Not yet. We need everyone inside the compound, save god.

Leave god outside on the porch. We will rest easy here while I go into the dark to find their captains.

The federales have us encircled. But which federales. Alphabet soup . . . 26 to choose from. Or is it the Hebrew alphabet? 27.

I think it's the NSA but it could be the DOJ; they've been wanting a show trial.

Some Iowans don't even know what's happened to their state.

Rachel and I have our night vision and our radios; but sometimes it is better to just look in the dark. The spirits will listen to you. And then, if a battery fails, you will still be alive.

How many to kill?

I count ten gunmen.

But we can't kill them all.

Pick two.

The man who looks like your father?

Or the one who looks like Don Juan?

The one with a beard?

Him.

Beard.

Rachel takes the skinny one.

Yes, *Enceiderich* but not *jetzt oder nicht*, but eternally. As long as you live. Decide and then decide again. and then again.

Fire.

134.

Why did the Jews become the pariahs of the world? It is a singular accomplishment. One so duly worked at. This spectacular stubbornness. This unreasoning regret in the face of change: to say:

"All right. I'll do part of it. But none of the rest. Don't ask me again."

But always we are asking them. Jews, what is it? What now? Jews, why? Please, Jews, help me to understand? Why do you refuse?

"It is my duty. My honor. My love. In refusal, I am reminded I am a man. I can still say no, whatever happens. So, no. And no."

Say no, and become a Jew. I have been a Jew for so long. Before I even knew what they were.

135.

You can do it too, you know. This is the most terrible lesson of all. You too are a trained killer. It's why you're here. Descendant.

136.

"This is not my Israel," she whispers.

"It's the one you wanted."

"We're not wanted here."

"Yes, you are."

"I'm going back."

"To do what?"

"To live."

Part 6
Peace

137.
The most dangerous one of all.
Peace in the Middle East.
Like peace in the human heart.
What could it mean?

\- - -

Peace is from *pag*, "to fasten." Related to *pacisi*, "to covenant or agree." As in pact.

This word replaced the Old English *sibb*, which also meant happiness.

The Peace from the Middle East came in, you see.

\- - -

We know peace is governed by agreements between rulers. So too are all modern religions founded on the ancient submissions steles of regional potentates to pharaoh.

Mossad has agreed to a transnational authority over Palestine/ Israel. They have actually relinquished their independence for an independence within.

Eastern Iowa shall be a kind of demilitarized zone for the first time since the Indian Wars; no one in or out.

Religion too makes a fetish of withdrawal from the world: the ascetics, and the practice of ritual purity, and various other theological strongholds obsessed with the dirt and dishonor of the world. Withdraw to god, and clean rooms.

Quantum physicists—many of them—now suspect gravity may be the one fundamental force whose origin lies external to this universe; it does not appear to be subject to the same laws as the others.

Gravity too withdraws from this world.

I, too; with this woman. But Mathilda will not come.

Perhaps I will no longer be a man.

- - -

Fasten your fastnesses and make ready for peace.

138.

War crimes tribunals are afoot. Who did what. Why did you do these things. Kill men, women and children. Obliterate neighborhoods. Destroy cities. Torture and harry and fight, tooth and nail, with your tails in the air, hair on fire, eyes mad, ritual embodiment of the world, thou shalt not withdraw, thou art in it, holy fury, midnight sun.

I am to be interviewed by the United Nations.

139.

China, the United States, France, Russia, and the United Kingdom. Their submission stele the modern religion of the world, bright beautiful and shining, in its thousand flags.

But I am not in New York; only in their regional Jerusalem office.

One arm of the government trying to outdo the other; shame them for the war they wanted, and the one they didn't.

Both the CIA and Mossad are in agreement, Rachel tells me. I will not be the sacrifice. It will be a Palestinian. Yet another whipping boy in this undying saga.

Like the central tenet of Christianity: sacrifice one of your own, for freedom.

140.

Freedom is related to friend. And to lover. It has nothing to do with choice, but with other people. You are free only with others.

141.

Rachel is sitting on Karaites street, sipping her coffee. I with her.

Black dove black ewe. What is in these eyes; like the eyes of a chimpanzee, dark and dark.

Like life, or loam. Black as the beach.

The heaviness passes over me like a fluid; gravity doing its work. The city remembering me, or one of my ancestors.

I know why she won't leave. All those old gods are still here, dying in laughter and solemn appreciation of our moronic sport, and our fierce determination, in living.

142.

"What is peace in the human heart, Rachel?"

"It's being alive. Just being alive."

Black dove, in thy finery, wash away, swim into the sand. I am Bedouin.

I am the sheikh, and you shall be a sayyadina among us, you already are.

Sayyadina.

Black ewe.

I am the meadow.

Eat me!

I am grass!

Eat me!

I am a river of wind; flowing over your wool.

I am the sun; shining around you.

I am the little world, behind the little Kabbalistic world, kept in your pocket, with your timepiece, I am your headpiece, I am your necklace, I am your companion.

Black ewe, stalwart as our walls, resplendent in the time from morning to sundown, and at night, a blanket, for my hands.

Woman; shine over the sun, I can see you, without any cedar, or fir, without lilies and without cherries or pomegranates, you are black against

the rays of the sun, cutting a star, by
day, to your mark, on the wall.
    "Come to bed, Robert, hmm?"
Black dove, you are shining.

Writer's Personal Thoughts

This is one of my more personal books for a couple of reasons. It marks a move away from science fiction for me—although likely I will never leave it entirely. Luckily I find that the "real world" is just as strange.

The love affair between the US and Israel is, in some ways, played out no more intimately than in Los Angeles. Here the great showman of the Jewish entertainer and the great rube of the honest American are conjoined in an ethnic and philosophical union, which, so far as I can tell, no man or god may put asunder.

Those who come to Los Angeles ignorant of these facts, as I did, are always in for rude awakenings.

In some ways, then, it is fair to consider this novel both my capitulation to the ruling cabals of Los Angeles, as well as my first real kick up its ass.

EDITORIAL

I tend to be with James Joyce, that the artist's job is to stand back from his completed work of art, paring his fingernails and saying nothing, but the nice thing about having a publisher is that the writer has, among other things, a first reader, someone to help puncture the solipsistic bubble Joyce championed.

The publisher has asked for my opinion about this book. Being a coward, I must try to answer an easier question instead: why did I choose to write the book?

To be honest, one reason I wrote it was to try to crawl back, like a defeated pirate, into the warm bosom of Her Majesty's Vessel of Commercial Fiction. I was determined to write a book that had no interdimensional portholes, no aliens, no inexplicable and spontaneously ruptured identities or bodies, and no torturous psychic phenomena (all tropes I've used, more than once, in my previous books).

Of course, I am sure that I have failed. One of the central tenets of commercial, realist fiction does seem to remain attached to the Enlightenment myth of the unified self, the Cartesian 'I' set against the world — this despite the efforts of more than a century of writers to explode that myth (Andre Gide and Robert Musil come to mind, from the turn of the last century and nearly all the modernist poets and novelists following eagerly lobbed grenades into the self . . .)

Well, anyway; there are no aliens in this one.

There are many good reasons to write a story about the love affair between the USA and Israel, and about the strange dilemma Israel faces, as it finds itself implementing a Holocaust upon the Palestinian people, and the horror the Palestinians face, at having been abandoned by the world, and perhaps, to some degree, one another. A documentary I watched recently about Palestine described many of its children as having "lost the will to live."

Still, there are older traditions than Enlightenment-mode realism. The same authority which the mass killer Henry Kissinger and his followers routinely cited—Thucydides, for his realpolitick view of the motivations and tactics of nations at war—was also arguably an early postmodernist, in his viciously keen eye for the contradictions in the human soul. One of the tenets of commercial realist fiction—at least since Dickens—seems to be that any changes in character behavior need to be carefully couched and described to allow them room to move in their appointed arc, so that we can watch them change and understand the reasons for it. In at least one sense, this Enlightenment notion is anti-scientific, since quite often we have no idea at all about the causes of phenomena, nor do we always understand even exactly what it is we are looking at. Thucydides was true to this deeper truth: that Mankind does all kinds of crazy things, and doesn't always stop to puzzle out why, and he can switch on a dime from cuddling babies to crushing them under his boots, and not always with a discernible reason behind these actions.

Such a worldview is fundamentally chaotic, and one reason why reading Thucydides is so difficult: his cool, collected prose obscures the madness he is describing.

I am not as hard-nosed as Thucydides, though, and so I feel relatively certain that I have, in Black Dove, still made nods towards the Enlightenment traditions of character arcs, motivations, and change. But I also made a concerted effort to jazz up the action—to syncopate the narrative beat so as to arrest our ideas of certainty and coherence in the face of war and love. This may well be one of the underlying principles of 'magical' realism (and science fiction . . . though again, this one has no aliens!): that the hidden causes of reality are discernible, but only just, like a dream. No omniscient narrator — who after all, is only human — can ultimately claim to explain any cause completely.

I am routinely populating my stories with an alter-ego — a Robin or Robert — something I don't always do consciously but which I know has been a fond tradition in the 20th Century novel up to the present. Critics, perhaps justly, call this lazy, and I certainly know myself to be lazy. But I also believe I know myself best.

So here "I" go again, into the breach, through the miasma of story-telling, into the arms of strange women and strange gods, in strange landscapes (with no aliens!) where no one can tell us, ultimately, what it means.

I hope you enjoy (or have enjoyed!) this story.

Robin Wyatt Dunn's Bio

Robin Wyatt Dunn's parents met at Teton National Park, and he was born there in Jackson. Robin writes and teaches in Los Angeles.